What His Heart Never Told Me

Some secrets live on, even after goodbye

Pairlee McGowan

Wichita, Kansas

Scripture quotations marked taken from the 1611 King James Version of the Bible. Public Domain.

Title: *What His Heart Never Told Me*
Subtitle: *Secrets live on, even after goodbye*
Author: Pairlee McGowan
Written: June 19, 2025
Published by: Leslie Light House, LLC

Disclaimer:

This book is a work of creative nonfiction. While inspired by true events from the author's life, it includes fictionalized scenes, characters, and dialogue for narrative purposes. Some names and identifying details have been changed to protect the privacy of individuals. Any resemblance to actual persons, living or dead, or actual events is coincidental and unintended unless explicitly stated by the author.

Dedication

I dedicate this book to my family, friends, and church family, who have supported me every step of the way. I thank my family, especially my granddaughter Shay, for encouraging me to keep writing when I wanted to stop. I also thank Ms. Stephanie Stovall, who helped me turn my manuscript into the pages of this book. I thank God for her assistance. It has been a challenge, but I did not give up. Thank you all.

Table of Contents

CHAPTER 1

A New Beginning

My children and I left for New York, and I never looked back. We love it here. I have found a job that does not pay very much, but we are happy. That is why when I look back and see where God has brought me from, I cannot help but rejoice in the glory of His goodness and praise Him.

He has brought me a long way. He has blessed me with a better home in which to live. He has blessed me so much that I cannot put it into words. So, what else can I ask for?

When we moved to New York, I met three women and their husbands. Two of them lived across the street from me, and we all worked together. We became like sisters, best friends. Their names are Kathy, whose husband is Robert; Doris, whose husband is Frank; and Sandra, whose husband is David. Ever since I arrived here, and they learned that I'm divorced, they have been trying to hook me up with a guy. I do not have a social life. I just commute to work and back home because of my previous marriage.

My friends think I should go out and meet someone. "No, thank you," I would say. I did not want to repeat the same mistakes. My friend Sandra told me that I'm a person who gets along well with everyone. The reason I'm not dating anyone is that I don't get out or put myself out there and flirt with the guys. Why would I do that to find a man? When you smile and speak to them, they think you want to be with them, despite what your intentions are. "Don't you think so?" I asked her. Sandra has been happily married for a long time, and she and her husband have three grown children and four grandchildren.

I told her, "Girl, you know I'm not going to throw myself at any man, never."

"And that's why you aren't dating anyone, my friend."

"Well, Sandra, the choice is mine whether or not I want to begin dating anyone."

"Okay, Susie, now you're angry with me?"

"No, I'm not angry, Sandra, but I need to do this my way, and, in my time, I'm not ready to date anyone right now, maybe never."

My friends do not understand just how badly my marriage ended. My ex-husband, Josh, put me through a great deal. I thought I was going to lose my mind. I cannot go through that again.

After my experience with Josh, I turned my life over to God and nothing else really

matters to me. With God, I can't go wrong. He will not hurt me and I can trust Him in all things. It's good to have someone to lean on and depend on. Yes, I have friends, and I love them all. Friends leave, they change, and they're not always there when I need them. But God is a friend for life. There's no better friend to have than a friend in Jesus. I've always believed in God, but I lacked the faith and confidence to act on that belief.

One part of faith is giving God a tenth of your earnings. I have no objection to doing that, but Josh did not feel that way. I asked my pastor, Dr. Dennis, about what I should do in that case. He told me that, yes, God requires us to give a tenth of our earnings; however, since you are not working and your husband provides you with money for your bills, that's what you should do with the money- especially since his faith is not as strong as yours.

After I divorced Josh, I found that despite having a job and earning my own income, I was still unable to cover all my expenses or pay my tithes due to the frequent bills that required payment. But I kept remembering what God said in His word. "If you do this, He will pour out a blessing that I would not have room enough to receive." But it was hard when the bill collectors were knocking on my door.

> **Malachi 3:10 says, *"Bring ye all the tithes into the storehouse, that there may be meat in mine house, and prove me now herewith, said the LORD of hosts. If I will not open the windows of heaven and pour you out a blessing, that there shall not be room enough to receive it."***

I'm wrestling with this scripture, and God keeps saying, "Put your trust in Me so that I can prove Myself to you." Paying my tithes instead of a bill and trusting God to take care of the rest - it was hard. I'm having trouble applying it to my life, yet I continue to pray that I will learn to step out on His word. It's all about having that mustard seed faith, to put it all in God's hand, and let Him prove Himself to me.

CHAPTER 2
Meeting My Fiancé

When I got home from work today, there was a message on my phone. It was my neighbor. She told me she had met a guy while jogging in the park and thought I would like to meet him. Oh my God - whatever gave her the idea that I would want to meet someone she met in the park? My friends keep trying to hook me up with somebody. First Sandra and now Doris - give me a break. They're tired of me tagging along solo with them and their husbands. Well, I can certainly stay at home.

The next morning, when I got to work, Doris came into my office to tell me all about this guy she met in the park.

"No, no, I don't want to hear anything about some guy that you met in the park," I told her.

Oh girl, he's really handsome and very nice."

"Look, Doris, I'm not ready to meet anyone right now. First Sandra, and now you, what's going on?" I asked her.

"But Susie, I know you will like him. He is single. His wife passed away a few years ago, and he's not dating anyone. I know you will like him."

"Please! And you learned all this from a jog in the park from a stranger?"

"Girl, you know that if I want to know something, I just ask. We want you to be happy, Susie, and get back into the swing of things. We love you, and you're our best friend."

After work, while I was cooking dinner, I couldn't stop thinking about what Doris had said. I'm hung up on protecting my heart from being broken. Having a man in my life was the farthest thing from my mind. But the more I thought about what she told me, the more I felt that this may very well be my last chance to be happy. Mama said to us that whenever we were unsure about things, when we needed answers, "Go to God." So, I couldn't leave God out of my decision, because He's my anchor. I've always tried to consult Him in everything - through prayer and His words. Mama taught us kids to do that.

Ring, ring. Oh, that must be Doris.

"Hello."

"Hey girl, it's all set for you to meet John on Friday."

"What on earth do you mean, it's all set - and who is John?"

"The guy I met in the park. His name is John Barter, and he agreed to have dinner with Kathy, Robert, Frank, and me. He would very much like to meet you, and we didn't want you to go alone."

"Oh, that was sweet of you. I'm not sure if I'm ready for this."

"Oh, honey, it'll be all right, you'll see.

"I don't even know what I'd wear to this travesty you have planned for me. It's been a long time since I've been on a date, especially with someone that I don't know."

"Kathy and I will help you find something perfect to wear."

"Well, that's the least you can do for putting me in the middle of this mess."

It's Friday, and all day I couldn't stop thinking about this dinner date and what I had gotten myself into with my friends. That night, as I got dressed while looking in the mirror, I thought to myself; "Girl, you do look good." When I arrived at the restaurant, I could feel my body trembling. I hoped that he didn't notice. Doris introduced everyone to John.

"John Barter, this is Susie Cane."

"Hi, Susie. Glad to meet you. I've heard so much about you." (Yes, I'm sure you have, I thought.) John inquired extensively about my family.

He said, "Doris told me that you're divorced and have three children - boys or girls?" (Oh, she didn't tell you that, I thought.).

"Yes, I am divorced. I have two sons and a daughter. What about you?"

"I'm a widower. My wife passed away three years ago."

"Oh, I'm sorry," I told him.

"Thank you! I have two children, a boy and a girl. My daughter has a little boy."

"Oh, so you're a grandpa?"

"Yes, my son Stanley is in college."

"Wonderful. My daughter, Valerie, recently had a beautiful little girl. My son, Greg, has a son. My son, Thomas, doesn't have any children - he's away in college."

"All right, that's enough about the kids. Let's dance," Kathy said.

"Susie, may I have this dance?" John asked. My legs felt like Jell-O - he was holding me so close. Oh Lord, please give me strength. A man hasn't held me since I can't even remember. Frank suggested that we all go to their place for a nightcap.

"Is that all right with you, John?"

"Sounds good to me, if Susie will join me."

"Yes, I'd love to," I told him.

"Would you like to ride with me, Susie?" John asked.

"Well, I have my car."

"Gosh, Susie, loosen up a little. We'll pick up your car in the morning," Doris said.

"I'm loose, big mouth."

We all laughed. When John took me home, he gave me a very gentle kiss on the cheek and said goodnight.

"Susie, maybe we can do this again sometime."

"Yes, I'd love that. Goodnight."

Doris was right. John is a hunk and very polite. He really knows how to treat a lady. That's something that I wasn't used to. I don't know why I hadn't moved on with my life - scared, I guess. Yet, if someone like John had come along before, it would have made all the difference in my attitude toward men and my fear of getting hurt.

> **Exodus 14:13 :*"...Fear ye not, stand still, and see the salvation of the Lord, which He will shew to you today..."***

Early the next morning, Doris came to pick up my car. She's so nosy and was probably looking out her window when John dropped me off last night.

"Well, Susie, what did you think about John?"

"Doris, for God's sake, I just met the man. What can I say?"

"Come on, Susie, I know you have an opinion. Don't you?"

"All right, he's a hunk. Like you said, he's incredible. I think I could really fall for him. Is that what you wanted to hear?"

"That's my girl. I knew you would like him. Did he ask you out again?"

"Not yet, but he said he'd love to sometime. Ok?"

The service on Sunday morning was very good. The pastor spoke about love - if you can believe that? He said Jesus Christ was all about love, and that's what He teaches us. Love is one of God's greatest commandments: to love your neighbor as you love yourself, and we know that God's love surpasses all knowledge. His love is so great that we cannot fully understand it.

I felt great after church. I went home, fixed a big dinner, and invited my children over. We talked about John.

Valerie asked, "Mother, are you falling for this John?"

"Honey, I could easily fall for him. He is unbelievable. I have never met anyone quite like him, but I would like to get to know him better."

Monday morning, as soon as I got to work, Doris and Kathy came over to put me through the third degree. They have great husbands, which is why they will not leave me alone. They think I should be happy because they are happily married. Everyone should be so lucky. Kathy's husband is all right - but he has a wandering eye - although he wouldn't act on it. Doris has a great husband - which is why she is such a pest. Sandra has a great husband, too.

After a stressful day, I decided to take a walk in the park, where I ran into John, who was sitting on a park bench.

"Well, hello there, looks like you're really relaxing."

"Hello there, beautiful. I was thinking about you."

"Yes, I've been thinking about you as well. Come on, let's take a walk."

"I've been wanting to call to see if you'd like to have dinner with me."

"Well, why haven't you?"

"Would Saturday be a good time for you?"

"Yes, Saturday would be great."

"Ok, I'll pick you up at seven."

"I will be ready."

We walked and talked hand in hand around the park until the sun had gone down, not realizing what time it was. He walked me home, and I invited him in for a cold drink.

"Oh, John, I am having a potluck dinner. You're welcome to stay."

"Sounds great. I would love to."

After dinner, John helped me clean up the kitchen, and we talked for a while. Finally, he said, "I had better go. I have an early morning appointment. Everything was lovely - thanks for dinner." He kissed me on the cheek as he said goodbye. As I looked up, I saw Doris looking out her window - Ms. Nosy. I was already nervous about what to wear on Saturday night because I wanted to look nice.

Saturday night was wonderful. John and I had a great steak dinner and a bottle of wine at Sauté. After dinner, we went to a movie. I could not tell you what the movie was about. John had his arms around me so tightly I could barely breathe - let alone remember the movie. He took me home and said good night. He has been a perfect gentleman each time we have been together. It is very unusual not to have a man pawing all over you on the second date. We are getting close. I can feel it in my heart. God knows I did not want to rush and make the same mistakes I made with my ex-husband, so I like the slow pace we're taking.

On Wednesday, I attended Bible study as usual. Afterward, I talked to my Pastor about John.

He said, "Susie, you've been hurt so badly that you're not willing to risk your heart to another. Reclaim your broken heart child and love again. Pray and ask God to guide you. He will give you the answers you need. So, daughter, follow your heart."

"Pastor, you know my heart has been sitting on a shelf for a long time, collecting dust. I'm afraid, but I think I'm falling in love with this man."

"Bring that fellow by. I want to meet him, Susie."

"All right, pastor, I'll do that."

John called to tell me that he had to go out of town and would be away for a week, but he wanted to see me as soon as he got back. "All right, I'll be waiting, but I'll miss you." I think my heart has fallen off that dusty shelf. I'm in love. My workweek seems to have stood still missing John.

CHAPTER 3

My Sister's Visit

Leslie, my sister, called me. She sounded upset and asked if she could come for a visit.

I told her, of course you can. She said she needed to talk to me.

"Can you pick me up from the airport at six o'clock?"

"Oh, my love, I'll be there. Honey, is everything all right?"

"I'll tell you about it when I get there on Friday evening." I hoped everything was all right with her and Bradley.

Leslie's plane was on time. I knew she wanted to talk to me, but John was coming home on Saturday, and I wanted to see him so badly. However, my sister needed me. We talked for hours. She said that Brad was having an affair, and he told her it was her fault.

"Oh, honey, he's got his nerves. Don't let him blame you for his indiscretions; he's the one who broke his marriage vows. I don't understand why these men try to blame their wives when they mess up."

"He said that he needed someone who would be around when he needed them, and not working all the time. I do have to work," Leslie said.

"My sweet sister, does he want you to quit your job, stay home, and cater to his every need? Don't quit your job. He's cheating on you, and he wants you to become dependent on him. You will probably need your job. Don't let him get away with treating you that way, because he will continue, unless you stop him.

> **Hebrews 13:4 says, "*Marriage is honorable in all, and the bed undefiled: but whoremongers and adulterers God will judge.*"**

We must understand that one day, we will all give an account of our actions before God.

Ring, ring - that's probably my baby!

"Hello, oh, you're back."

"Yes, and I'm on my way to your house. I can't wait to see you."

"Ok, I'll see you in a few. My sister Leslie's here, honey."

"Oh, I don't want to interrupt your visit with your sister."

"Oh, that's all right. She wants to meet you, and we've been talking all night. Have you eaten anything?"

"No, I haven't."

"Do you mind stopping to get us some Chinese takeout, please?"

"I certainly will. See you soon."

"Susie, I can't wait to meet your fellow," Leslie said.

«I know you will like him; he's one of a kind."

A few minutes later, John arrived.

"Oh, come in John. I want you to meet my sister Leslie. John, this is Leslie. Leslie, this is John."

"It's great to meet you. I've heard so much about you, John."

"Likewise, it's good to meet you as well."

"Les, John travels to so many different places on his job. He's a site inspector for his company."

"Oh, that sounds like fun, traveling all over."

"Yes," John said. "It is sometimes, but since I met your sister, I'd rather be here spending time with her. I'm going to take her with me one day soon."

"All right now," Leslie said. "All work and no play," we all laughed.

Ring, ring, who could that be?

"Hello? Hi Kathy, how are you?"

"Oh, I'm fine, Susie. I just called to tell you who I just ran into? You remember Bob, who works at Conner gas station? Well, he's fooling around with Connie's sister, Cora."

"Oh my God, are you kidding me? Girl, I can't believe he cheated on his beautiful wife, Francis. I saw her at church on Sunday. She's such a gracious lady. Why would he do that to her? Oh my goodness, are you sure? What's wrong with these men? I hope she never finds out."

Proverbs 18:22 says, *"Whoso findeth a wife findeth a good thing, and obtaineth favour of the Lord."*

Sunday morning, John, my sister, and I went to church. My Pastor was impressed by John and told him, "Now don't you mistreat my girl; you hear? You seem like a fine young man."

"I most certainly won't, Sir," John told him.

"Mrs. Leslie, it's clear that you two are sisters. It's nice to meet you. How long will you be staying?" Pastor asked.

"Thank you, sir. It's nice to meet you as well. I will be here until this evening."

The Pastor told John, "You come back to visit real soon."

"Yes, Sir, I would love to."

I said, "Next Sunday, I'm going to church to meet his Pastor, Reverend Falconer.

CHAPTER 4
Falling In Love

When I got to work Monday morning, Kathy was the first person I went to see.

"Hello, Kathy. How was your weekend? I didn't see you outside the entire weekend. You ok?"

"I am great. I got a great deal done, plus had time for myself."

"So, why didn't you come over?"

"Well, every time I looked over, you had company."

"Yes, my sister came for a brief visit, and John got back into town. I didn't see either of you at church on Sunday."

"Well, I didn't feel good over the weekend, and I don't feel good today," Kathy said. Doris chimed in, "Girl, you should have stayed home."

"Yes, Doris. I know, but I need the money, so I can't miss too many days."

"Girl, I heard that."

"We need to get to work before we won't have a job. But first, let me tell you what happened at church. John met Pastor Berry."

"Well, how did that go?" Kathy asked.

"It went well, but Pastor Berry told John that he'd better take good care of his girl."

"No, he didn't," Doris said."

"Yes, he did! But John said he liked him, and he really enjoyed the service."

"After church, we went to dinner. Then we drove Leslie around the lake, got out, walked, and talked about our families. John told us he has two brothers who live in Michigan. He told them he had met a wonderful lady. "

"Oh, did he now?" said Doris.

"Yes, Doris. I asked him if he thought they would like me, and he said, 'They had better, because he loved me.' I told him I loved him too."

"My sister said, 'Oh well, is there going to be a wedding?"

"I never thought those words would ever cross my lips again. Girls, I love him very much. That's all I'm going to say."

"Well, congratulations, we're happy for you."

All I could think about was his deep brown eyes staring into mine when he said he loved me. Later, I found myself unable to say one word as he kissed me so passionately. When we arrived at my house, I asked John if he had any sisters. He said, "No, just us hardheaded boys. My brothers are both married to wonderful women. Benjamin's wife is Joyce, and Charles's wife is Mary. They don't have any children, but Benjamin and Joyce have three children. I haven't seen them in a while. Maybe we can take a trip out there to see them soon."

"Oh, that sounds great," I told him. "In my family, there are three of us. You met Leslie. We have a brother, Herbert. He lives in Texas. His wife is Christine, and they have three children. He's upset with me and, I haven't talked to or seen him since Mama died. One day, he'll come around, because we're family. We have this hope as a secure anchor, which binds us together, no matter the circumstances - we are one in the blood.

"I'm sorry, baby," John said. "I can see you're upset because of this. But keep praying that it'll be all right."

"My mother's brother and sister still live in Kansas. I have a lot of cousins who live there, whom we haven't seen since our parents died. We didn't visit often, and I'm not sure why. My parents were loners and not particularly family-oriented."

Leslie said, "Ok, that's enough about our families. I've really enjoyed my time here with you, Sis, and meeting your guy."

"Oh, honey, it's been wonderful having you here. It's time to get you to the airport, so you don't miss your flight. I hate seeing you leave, and I'm praying that you and Bradley will be all right."

On the way back from the airport, John said, "I would like to take you on a long weekend for some much-needed R and R. Just the two of us, let me pamper you."

"Where are we going, and when, I asked?"

"Maybe to Las Vegas, see a show, whatever you want."

"Oh, I can't wait."

"Well, just let me know the best time for you to get away. I'll make the arrangements. You pack your bag, and off we'll go," John said.

"I'll do that tomorrow," we both laughed.

CHAPTER 5
Meeting John's Pastor

I attended John's church on Sunday. He has a huge church, and his pastor is very nice. He told John, "I'm happy you have met someone to love."

"Ms. Cane, you've got yourself a wonderful young man. He's a God-fearing man and he works very hard in the church. I hope you're not going to sway him over to St. John."

"Oh no, Reverend, I'd never do that."

Reverend Falconer introduced me to his lovely wife. She's a special lady - no wonder John loves them. She invited me to visit again and to have John bring me for dinner sometime.

She said, "I think you're going to be around for a long time," we all laughed. I thought to myself, you're right if I have anything to say about it.

CHAPTER 6

My Friend Loses Her Son

When I got home, Doris and her children came over. I hadn't seen her children in a while - they have really grown up. "Justin has grown so tall," Doris said, "that he's now playing basketball at school." I told Justin to let me know when he's playing. John and I would love to come and watch him play.

Ring, ring.

"Hello. How's my baby girl? How's everyone? I haven't heard from you or the boys in a while."

"We're fine, Mama. Who's over there?"

"Well, Doris, her children, and John. We just got back from John's church and dinner." "Oh, how did you like his church?"

"It's huge. I met his Pastor and wife. They're very nice."

"Where did you go to dinner?"

"We went to Hometown Bar-B-Que."

"Where were you last Sunday? I didn't see you at church?"

"Lazy Mama, but we were there today. I was wondering where you were. Now I know you were at John's church. Mom, I'll let you get back to your guest. I'll talk to you later."

"All right, honey, kiss my baby girl for me."

"Sorry, that was my daughter."

"Doris, have you heard from Kathy this weekend? Did you go to church today?"

"Yes, we did, and Kathy was there."

"Susie, baby, I'm going to go so you can enjoy your company."

"Ok, baby, but I enjoy your company, too."

"I know, honey, but I have a hard day tomorrow, and I need to get some rest. I'll call you before bedtime, all right."

"Yes, you better. Bye. Love you."

"Good night, Doris. It was great seeing you again."

"Likewise, John."

"Are you ready for work tomorrow, Doris?"

"I guess, might as well be. You know I haven't heard anything more about Bob and Cora. I've been praying for his wife."

"My goodness, I didn't tell you my guy wants to take me on a holiday."

"Where's he taking you?"

"To Vegas, to see a show, and to shop.

"Aha! He might ask you to marry him. So, what did you tell him?"

I said, "When tomorrow?"

"Girl, you are crazy, but it could happen. He could ask you to marry him. We always told you that the two of you were meant for each other."

"Yes, you all did. I was the one doubting you had faith, but it's just for the weekend."

Psalm 118:8: *"It is better to trust in the Lord than to put confidence in man."*

Yet, I had to pray that God would direct me in the right way. So whatever He chooses - so may it be - because in Him I put all my trust.

When I got home from work Monday evening, there was a message from my friend Sandra. I was feeling bad because I hadn't called her in a long time. She had told me she needed to talk to me as soon as I got home. I could tell that she had been crying, so I became really concerned and called her right away. Sandra told me that her son, Robert Jr., had been in a serious accident and was not doing well. As she began to cry, I told her that I'd be right there. "Oh Lord, let that young man be ok," I prayed as I drove to the hospital.

When I arrived at the hospital, I was trembling. My emotions were all over the place. "Oh God," I said, "let me calm down before I reach my friend." When Sandra looked and saw me, she ran and fell on her knees. How could I comfort her? I held her and prayed silently as she told me what happened to her son, explaining that the doctors had done all they could. "My friend, God has the last word about this; let's pray." So we all gathered around, arm in arm, and began to pray. It's in His hands now. I called my son, Greg, because he and Robert had gone to college together. I knew he would want to be here, and he came right over.

We kept vigil all night, and in the early morning, Sandra and David lost their baby boy. It was so sad thinking about how they must have felt, putting myself in their place, and visualizing how I would have felt if it were one of my sons. Oh, Lord, they were devastated - probably asking, "Why our baby?" and thinking, "We were supposed to die before our child." Still, we must keep in mind that God has no respect of person, age, creed, or color. It's His call, and He made it. But it's hard to realize that when you're in so much pain.

We were all tired, so we went home. I called my daughter to let her know what had happened and to ask her to come help prepare food for the family. She said, "Mom, you need to call John. He's so worried because he couldn't reach you, and I couldn't reach Greg either."

"Oh, honey, I'm so sorry. We had to turn off our phones and forgot to turn them back on. I'll call him right away."

"Hello baby, I'm so sorry that I didn't call to let you know what happened. Do you remember me telling you about my friend Sandra and her husband David? I haven't introduced them to you yet, but their son Robert was hurt in a car accident yesterday and passed away this morning.

"Oh no, honey, you should have called me."

"Yes, I know, but when Sandra called me, I wanted to get to her as soon as possible."

"I understand, but you shouldn't have been driving while you were that upset. Please don't do that again; call somebody. I was so worried that anything might happen to you. Oh, no, I don't even want to think about it! Please don't do that again - I love you so much."

"No, I won't. I will call you or someone, no matter what."

"Valerie will be over to help me fix food for the family, but I need to shower first. I'll talk to you later."

"Yes, you will. I'll be right over. Do you need me to bring anything?"

"Yes, honey, if you don't mind, please bring two loaves of bread, sodas, plates, and napkins. Thank you, baby, I'll see you soon." I wondered if Sandra and David's other children had been notified.

They have another son who attends medical school and a daughter who lives in California.

Psalm 25:1: "*Unto thee, Oh Lord, do I lift up my soul to you.*"

Robert's funeral was Friday morning. It was understandably heartbreaking - so much sadness and sorrow. I could not help but think about his wife and little son, Lord. I just wanted to scoop them up in my arms and hold them tight, praying, "Lord, please be with them - not just for today, but every day from now on."

"John, honey, I promise to stay in touch with my friends. I feel bad that I haven't spoken to Sandra in over a month. I feel terrible about that."

"Baby, I am sure she understands. She called when she needed you, and she knows you care about her."

"I do, John. I love them and their children as if they were my own."

"I'm taking you home," John said, "so you can lie down and get some rest. You are tired and upset, aren't you?"

"Yes, I'm tired and didn't get much sleep last night."

"That settles it. You get some sleep; you can check on Sandra later. When you wake up, I'll be downstairs."

Later, when I woke up, I called Sandra. David answered and said she was sleeping. I asked him to tell her, "I called to check on you all and see if you needed anything."

"Yes, I will tell her - and thanks for calling, Susie."

Romans 12:15: *"Rejoice with them that do rejoice, and weep with them that weep."*

Thank God it is Saturday. I'm going to do a little housecleaning, laundry, get myself together for church tomorrow, and call my boys to see if they're all right. Doris came over, and we spent a long time talking. "This has been a trying week," I told her. "Yes, it has, girl," she said, "Maybe we can catch a break."

> **Psalm 138:8: "*The Lord will perfect that which concerneth me: thy mercy, O Lord, endureth forever: forsake not the works of thine own hands.*"**

John called to tell me he was on his way over with lunch and a cool drink for me - as if I needed it. He's always trying to do something thoughtful for me, and I am thankful to the Lord for sending this wonderful man into my life. Most importantly, he doesn't push me in any way. He shows me unconditional love and respect, and asks for nothing in return.

Ring, ring.

"Hello, Sandra, how are you? Are you getting any rest?"

"Susie, I'm feeling much better after taking a nap; I was so tired. Thanks for checking on us."

"Yes, of course, Love. When are your children leaving?"

"They are leaving Monday morning. I hate to see them leave, but I know they must get back to their lives."

"I know you do, Sandra. Call me if you need anything anytime. If I am unavailable, please call Valerie to discuss or address any concerns. How is David doing? Is he all right?"

"Yes, he's doing fine. Tell your friend John hello for me, and thank him for all his help." "Yes, I will. We'll have to get together soon so I can introduce him to you all." "Thanks, Susie. I'm looking look forward to that."

When I got home from church on Sunday, my brother Herbert had called. All I could do was cry. I had not heard from him since our mother passed. He was so angry with me that he left without even saying goodbye. Oh, my goodness, I love him so much. Maybe he called to make amends - I have been praying for that. I need to call right now; life is too short to be in a family feud.

"Hello Christine, this is Susie."

"Oh my God, Susie! How are you doing? Herbert told me he called you. I'm so happy he did. Let me get him for you."

"Hello, my Susie girl. I'm so glad that you called me back. I thought maybe you wouldn't."

"Herbert, I was so happy to hear from you. Oh my goodness, I've been praying for this day. Are you all right? Is anything wrong?"

"No baby, nothing's wrong. I just needed to talk to you. Leslie told me that she had come to visit you a while back. I told her that I'd be calling you. It's time to let go of all this mess so that we can be family again."

"I love you so, so much, Herbie. Thanks for calling me. I've missed you so much. I've wanted to call you many times. Oh, I have some good news. I've met a wonderful man. Oh, Herbie, I've fallen in love. He's so different from anyone I've ever met."

"That's wonderful, Sis. How are the children and the grands?"

"Everyone's great. How about your children?"

"Everyone's fine. You have made me so happy today, on a Sunday, of all days. I praise God! Tell everyone I love them all and I love you. I'm going to say goodbye, before I cry. I love you, sis. Goodbye."

Psalm 75:1 : "*Unto thee, O God, do we give thanks, unto thee do we give thanks: for that thy name is near thy wondrous works declare.*"

All I can say is, "Thank you, God." I felt so rejuvenated and complete. *Ring, ring,* "Hello Sandra, how are you doing?"

"I am doing all right, Susie. I was calling to see if you could meet me for lunch tomorrow."

"Yes, I would love to. I can take a lunch break at either 12:00 or 1:00, whichever is more convenient for you."

"Make it 1:00. All right, I will see you at the park; it's close to your job."

"Okay, Sandra, I'll see you tomorrow. Bye, love." I had to wonder what was wrong with her; she sounded so serious. I hoped everything was all right.

After my call with Sandra, I called Doris. "Doris, Sandra called me this afternoon. She wants to meet me for lunch, so you and Kathy should go to the mall without me. I know we were going to check out the sales. If things go well with Sandra, then I'll meet you guys at the mall."

Doris wanted to know if I'd talked to Kathy. She wasn't at church yesterday and she hoped she was okay. I told her that I had spoken to Kathy on Saturday and I would check on her later.

Sandra and I met for lunch. I didn't know what to expect from her or why she was so adamant about talking to me today. "Hello, Sandra, how are you?"

"I'm doing okay, Susie. You're probably wondering why I insisted on talking to you today. I needed some advice, and you're the only one I can trust right now. I need to tell someone, or I'm going to lose my mind."

"Sandra, what on earth is wrong? You're scaring me?"

"Susie, I know this will come as a shock to you, but I've decided to leave David. I'm going to California to stay with my daughter for a couple of months."

"Oh no, girl! What are you talking about? Why do you want to leave your husband? What has he done to make you want to leave him?"

"It's been coming for a long time and after Robert's death, everything just came unraveled," she told me.

"I can't be with him any longer because he has been unfaithful to me with Sara Baker."

"How do you know this?"

"I caught them together a couple of days ago after our son's funeral. Susie, I know I haven't been there for him, and we grieved our son's death alone. I couldn't help him with his grief, and he couldn't help me. So, he turned to someone else. He said that I hadn't been there as a wife or anything else for a long time, and he was right. I haven't been there for him, Susie. I don't blame him for finding solitude elsewhere. Now it's just too late for us."

"Oh, Sandra, you need to talk to someone. What about Pastor Berry?"

"I don't know what to say."

"How long have you felt this way?"

"Probably two to three years before Robert's death."

"Do you want to give up on your marriage?" I asked. "Oh, my sweet girlfriend, I thought David and you were solid."

"We were Susie."

"Please, Sandra. Talk to someone before you leave him, please."

"I hate this. You know that I love you with all my heart."

"Yes, Susie, I know that you love me. I love you, too. Knowing that David has defiled our marriage, I can't go back to him. I don't know how long this has been going on."

"You didn't ask him?"

"No, I don't want to know."

"Oh, honey, I've got to get back to work, but we need to talk some more before you leave, all right?"

"I plan to leave on Wednesday morning. Why wait?" she said.

"You can't leave yet. Let me talk to him."

"No, Susie, I know you want to help, and I love you for it, but I've already decided I'm leaving the day after tomorrow."

"I'm going to pray very hard that you change your mind; stay and fight for your marriage."

"Thank you, my good friend. I will call you before I leave and when I'm settled.

On my way back to work, my mind was flip-flopping. I couldn't believe what was going on with my friends. We don't know what goes on in the privacy of people's homes. Here I am finding happiness in my life for the first time in many years. Yet, everything around me was falling apart. I found myself feeling a little nervous and asking myself if I should jump into another marriage. Should I put off being happy? Instead, should I hold onto my relationship with John for dear life?

When I got back to work, Doris said, "I see you didn't make it to the mall."

"No, Doris, I didn't see any good sales. Yes, I found a couple of pairs of pants and shirts."

:You seem a little down since you got back. What's wrong?" Kathy asked.

"I have some unsettling news, but I'd prefer not to discuss it right now."

:All right, we understand; maybe later."

I didn't feel like working the rest of the day. I was so upset about Sandra and David's situation, thinking about their children and how they would feel about their parents' separation after all these years.

I remember how my children felt after my separation. It's breaking my heart to see this happening to my friends. Sandra worked with Kathy, Doris, and me for a while. Then she just stayed home to raise her children, so we didn't see her very often.

When I got home from work, I called Sandra, but she didn't answer. I left a message for her to contact me. Wednesday came, and I still hadn't heard from her. I was so worried but I realized there are some things that we can't do anything about, so I just prayed. John called to see how I was doing. I knew he could perceive from the tone of my voice that things weren't going well. He asked me if I'd eaten. I told him that I hadn't, and he brought dinner. I couldn't tell him that I wasn't hungry; he'd be upset. When he got to my house, he said, "Honey, I know something's wrong. What is it?"

"You remember my friends David and Sandra?"

"Yes, I remember. What's wrong?"

"Sandra's leaving him to go live with her daughter - their marriage is over. I always thought they were happy, the perfect couple. She was always on me about finding love. Her leaving him is hard for me to understand."

CHAPTER 7
My Engagement

"Susie, this is why I need to get you away from here. You need the "R" and "R" I mentioned earlier; you need a break. Tomorrow, find out how long you can be off work, and I'll take care of the rest. I mean it - as soon as possible, all right?"

"Yes, I will do that."

Thank you, God, for this wonderful man. He is always trying to make me happy; he is just what I need in my life. I am so grateful for this blessing. When I arrived at work, I requested time off, and it was approved. My friends were excited for me; they were so sure he would ask me to marry him in Vegas - that's where I thought we were going. However, he changed his mind, and took me to Michigan to meet his brothers. I was excited, but nervous too.

We went to his brother Ben's house first. He was very likable, reminding me so much of John. His wife, Joyce, made us feel welcome in their beautiful home and made a lovely lunch for us. I felt like I was already a member of their family. Ben asked John, "So when is the big day?"

He said, "As soon as this beautiful lady says yes."

"Well, Susie, what's the holdup?" Joyce asked.

"I'm waiting for this wonderful man to ask me."

"That's forthcoming," John said.

Ben said, "So we're going to a wedding soon? It's good to see my brother so happy. He hasn't been this happy in a long time, Susie. He has met the right woman; we can tell. Isn't that right, Honey?" Ben said.

"He's right, Susie, John's in love for the first time since Jenna passed. Thank you for making my brother-in-law happy again."

"Thanks, Joyce. He knows I love him, and he has made me a happy woman as well. My children and friends are crazy about him."

I really couldn't believe John surprised me with a trip to meet his family. Ben called his children, Brenda and Steven, and they came over. "Hello, Uncle John, I haven't seen you in years," John's niece Brenda said.

"Hi, baby girl, you've grown up to be quite a lady. You're no longer my baby girl."

"That's right, Uncle John, I'm married and have a child of my own. How are Paul and Beth?"

"They're fine, Paul's still in college, and Beth's busy chasing her son Raymond. What have you been doing, Steven?"

"Oh, I'm working, Uncle, and taking classes at the Community University."

"That's great, Steven. Where's Ben, Jr.?"

"He's working. I know he'll want to see you. How long are you going to be here for?"

"We'll make a point of seeing him, Brenda's husband and son, before we leave. Guys, I want you to meet the love of my life. This is Susie Cane."

"Hello, Ms. Cane, it's a pleasure to meet you," Brenda said.

"Hello there, and please call me Susie."

"Ms. Cane (Susie), do you have any children?"

"Yes, I do. I have two sons, a daughter, and two grandchildren."

"Oh, how wonderful, maybe we'll get to meet them someday." Brenda said,

"Mom, Dad, we must take off now. We'll see you all later. Nice to meet you, Ms. Susie.

"Likewise, Steven and Brenda."

Ben called his and John's brother, Charles, and Charles's wife, Mary, to let them know we were on our way to their house. They were just as hospitable as Ben and Joyce. We talked for a long time, they showed us around town, and they took us to a nice seafood restaurant. I had a catfish dinner; it was the bomb. We had so much fun, but we were tired from the day, so we went back to our car.

We checked into our lovely motel. My baby had gotten double beds, and I knew he was thinking that I wouldn't understand why, so he tried to explain. "He said baby, you know I love you with all my heart, but I want our wedding night to be special, the way God intended it to be. I would like to take you in my arms and hold you all night long, but you know that our Lord and Savior frowns on sex before marriage, even though we have both been married before. We want to start the right way in this. I know you understand."

"Yes, I do understand, John, you're a sweet and wonderful man. I'm so touched by your sincerity, that's why I love you."

Then he got down on his knees and said, "Susie, my love, will you please spend eternity with me as my wife? Will you marry me?"

I was crying, "Yes, yes, my love, I will marry you." He put the ring on my finger, and we held each other for what felt like an hour.

Paul said, "I say therefore to the unmarried and widows, it is good for them if they abide even as I. But if they cannot contain, let them marry: for it is better to marry than to burn. 1 Corinthians 7:8-9

CHAPTER 8
My Surprise Trip

Early the next morning, before we left, we went to Ben and Joyce's house for breakfast. Everyone gathered there to say goodbye. Joyce asked me if John and I attended the same church, and if that's where we met.

"My goodness, you wouldn't believe how we met. Long story short, my girlfriend met John in the park while jogging. Keep in mind, she's the nosy, inquiring type. She got the scoop on him and brought it to me. 'Girl, you'll like him,' she told me. And I told her I didn't want to meet some guy you met in the park. The next thing I knew, she had set us up on a blind dinner date with him, our girlfriends, and their husbands. I guess the rest is history - we fell for each at first sight, the rest is ongoing."

"That's so sweet", Joyce said.

"That's right, it was love at first sight," John said, "and that's not all. I asked her to marry me last night, and she said yes."

Everyone screamed with joy. "I'm happy for you brother," Charles said.

Mary said, "Let me see your ring. Oh, it's gorgeous."

"Thanks, Mary, my baby has good taste. We called our children; they were elated. My daughter was crying and screaming so loudly that I had to take the phone from my ear. I told John she was happy. When he called his children, he got the same reaction. "Honey, he said, "they're already planning the wedding and setting the date.". We told them we would talk to them when we got home.

Later at the motel, John told me his reasoning for not sharing a bed with me before marriage. He said, "Baby, you know that I teach those young men classes at my church. How could I teach them the right way if I'm not living the life that I'm teaching them - what thus says the Lord, and living a life that's not pleasing to God. Honey, I love those young men. They all come from different backgrounds, and I try to teach them to the best of my ability; it's very important to me. They all have different needs - some come from broken homes, have been in gangs, have stolen, you name it. I try to teach them that through Jesus Christ they do not need to live that kind of life – killing, being defiant to their parents. I told them to consider how their actions dishonor God. I ask them to ask themselves when they're about to do these things, *"Is this something that God would be pleased with?"* I also tell them to study His word first and foremost - no one can deceive you or trick you into believing things that are not true.

"Honey, I didn't want to get all off into that now; I just wanted you to understand that I'm trying to be a good example for them and for myself, before God, and practice what I teach."

"Wonderful, Sweetheart, I never heard you speak like that from your heart with such fondness for those young men. I thank God for you, John Barter. Reclaiming my heart has turned out to be the best part of my life. Trusting in my Lord and Savior to lead me in the right direction and give me the right understanding, letting me know that all men are not alike. My God of love, peace, and joy - who understood just what I needed in my life."

Ephesians 5:17 ***"Wherefore be ye not unwise, but understanding what the will of the Lord is."***

The Lord of mercy has brought me so far, and I will not turn around. He has given me the spirit of forgiveness. He has restored my faith in man. Whatever I come up against, God has said in His word that He will give me the desires of my heart. I know that He will, because His word is true. As John and I are waiting to give ourselves to each other on our wedding night, though we know we may be tempted. As we wait, we remember how Satan tempted Jesus while in the wilderness.

1 Corinthians 10:13: ***"There hath no temptation taken you but such as is common to man: but God is faithful, who will not suffer you to be tempted above that ye are able; but will with the temptation also make a way to escape, that ye may be able to bear it."***

Over the last few days, we stuffed ourselves, and finally we were dropping off the rental car at the airport. John said, "I have one more surprise for you."

"Oh, I can't stand another surprise."

"Well, you'll love this one, because we're going to Texas."

"Oh, my John, you didn't. We're going to see my brother?"

"Yes, we are."

"I can't believe you did this."

"Well, you met my family, so it's time that I met yours before we get married."

"Thank you, thank you, I'm so happy."

"I always want to make you happy, my darling."

We left for Texas that evening to visit my brother, Herbert, and his family. It was good to see him. We embraced and cried for a long time before I finally came to my senses and introduced John to my family. "This is my fiancée, John Barter."

Herbert said, "Did you say fiancée?"

"Yes, John asked me to marry him last night."

"Can't you see how happy I am? He then surprised me with a trip to see you all, after we visited his brothers and their families in Michigan."

"John, look at all this food; I tell you, we've been eating like little pigs. We'll have to go on a diet when we get home. John's family had so much food."

"Everything has been great," John said, "and it's great to finally meet my Susie's family. I've already met your sister, Leslie, and I hope to meet even more of your family at our wedding."

"So, when is the wedding?" Christine asked.

"Well, we haven't gotten that far yet. We want you all to come, and if it were left up to our children, it would be planned when we get back," I told her.

Herbert asked, "How long you are staying?"

John said, "I wish we could stay longer, but we have to get back to work. Our plane leaves at nine in the morning."

We arrived home Thursday night, tired but rejuvenated. We checked in on our children on Friday morning. On Saturday, I did a little housework and got myself together for church. I'm not sure how the pastor found out we had gotten engaged. Of course, I need not wonder who told him; none other than my friend, and my daughter told her.

My pastor said, "I'm so happy to announce the engagement of Sister Cane to Brother Barter."

"Daughter," he said, "I'm so happy that God has blessed you with this wonderful and Godly young man. This is a good example of what can happen when you put your trust in Him. Brother Barter's a fine young man."

After church, we all got together at my daughter Valerie and her husband Michael's home for dinner to celebrate our engagement. I was telling John what Reverend Berry said in church.

"Really, honey, the same thing happened at my church," John said. "I later found out that my son, Paul, spilled."

"Well, you don't have to ask who spilled at my church, since Doris and I attend the same church," we all laughed.

CHAPTER 9

Our Marriage And Honeymoon

After dinner, when I got home, I called Sandra. David said she was out of town visiting their daughter. I was really hurt that she didn't call me. I'm going to continue praying for her and David, hoping she will reconsider what she's about to do. Yet, I understand planning to leave your husband is a hard decision to make.

When I got to work on Monday morning, everyone was congratulated me on my engagement. Of course, you know who told everybody. Later, John called to tell me that he had to go out of town and wanted to take me to lunch before he left. When he arrived at my workplace, everyone congratulated him. He asked, "How do these people know who I am?"

I told him, "Probably from the pictures I have on my desk. Baby, don't forget our friend works here and you know she can't keep her mouth shut." He laughed.

At lunch, John mentioned he was tired of having to travel out of town so often.

"Yes, honey, I know we'll just have to pray about it, maybe you can get another position, so you won't have to."

"You're right," he said. "I just remembered an opening will be coming available in a couple of months. I'm heading back to the office to submit my bid, because once we're married, I don't want to be away from you for even a second, let alone two or three days. I'll see you Thursday after work. Maybe we can fix a picnic basket and go down by the lake. Everything will be ready when you get off work."

"That sounds wonderful. I love you," I told him as we said goodbye.

The rest of the work week passed slowly, but I managed to get a lot done, both at work and at home. I hadn't had the chance to hang out with Kathy and Doris, so they came over Tuesday evening so we could catch up. I managed to write thank-you notes to John's family. I also called my sister Leslie to tell her about our engagement, but my brother Herbert had already told her my good news.

I called my uncle in Kansas. They were so thankful that I had finally found someone to love. I asked them about my cousins and their families. Uncle Fred is my mother's only brother. His wife is Aunt Doreen. My mom has only one sister, Aunt Martha, who also lives in Kansas. My dad has one brother, Uncle Frank, who lives in Missouri and is getting up in age. I was glad I got a chance to talk to him. I told him that my brother Herbert had given me his phone number - I was shocked that he remembered me.

He said, "Hi there, Susie Q. How is my favorite niece?"

I said, "Uncle Frank, do you remember me?"

"Girl," he said, "you know I'll never forget about you. Why haven't I heard from you?"

"Uncle, I just got your number."

"How is everybody in your family, Susie Q?"

"Uncle, everyone is doing great. My daughter, Valerie, has a little girl. My son, Greg, has a little boy. Tommy is in college and not married yet. Uncle Frank, I called to let you know that I am getting married. We have not set the date yet, but I hope you can come."

"That's wonderful, Susie Q, but you know I've gotten too old to travel."

"Yes, Uncle, I know, but I thought George or Gracie could bring you. I would love it if Aunt Doreen, Aunt Martha, and Uncle Fred could also come."

"How is Herbert and his family doing?"

"My fiancée and I were down in Texas last week. They are doing great."

"How about Leslie?"

"She's doing well, Uncle. I need to get off this phone, but I will be calling you again soon."

"All right, baby, bye now."

After John and I get married, I would like to take a trip back to Kansas, so he can see where I grew up. It is always good to go back to your roots to see how far God has brought you from.

John and I got married on June 25th. It was a blessed occasion - everything was beautiful. My dress featured silk roses on the bodice and along the train, accented with white pearls - I felt like a princess. My bridesmaids wore rose-colored dresses, and the men wore black tuxedos with rose-colored bow ties. My nieces, Fay and Tiara, were the flower girls, and also wore rose colored dresses. They walked slowly and carefully down the aisle with smiles from ear to ear.

Now, it was my turn. I walked slowly and deliberately down the aisle, with my son Greg's arm around me. I could see all our children on both sides, with tears in their eyes. I was finally face-to-face with

John - he looked so handsome - and my heart was beating out of my chest. As I listened to the vows, my eyes watered. My pastor, Reverend Berry, asked me to repeat after him, "Susie Cane, do you take John Barter to be your lawfully wedded husband?"

"Oh yes, I do," I said.

Then John's pastor, Reverend Falconer, asked John to repeat the same thing, and he answered, "Yes, I do."

Both of our pastors presided, saying, "By the power of Almighty God, we now declare that you are husband and wife."

Pastor Berry said, "Go ahead and kiss your bride." Everyone laughed.

The cake was to die for, and the reception was out of this world. Our children worked well together - that is a true blessing. They planned everything, and we are so thankful for them. God allowed the sun to shine on a beautiful day. We had a lovely union - all our children, grandchildren, siblings, and friends were there to celebrate our wedding with us. We also had nieces, nephews, and cousins in attendance. My uncles and aunties could not make the trip, but that was all right. We will never forget this glorious day, blessed by God, and the most beautiful part was that both our pastors performed our wedding ceremony.

CHAPTER 10

First Holiday As Husband And Wife

It was a blessing to spend our honeymoon in Hawaii - a gift from our children. We had the best time, spending a whole week lying on the sandy beach - it felt like heaven on earth. I could feel God's presence all around us - that's how I knew He blessed our marriage. I am still thanking God for where He has brought me from, to become this remarkable man's wife. Everything in my life seemed to be going wrong until I put God first. Now, all the windows He promised He would open were so expansive that I couldn't hold all His blessings. It overwhelms me.

When we returned home, our family and friends greeted us. They had planned a small welcome home celebration for us. Our children had moved all my things into John's house and transformed our bedroom into a little honeymoon suite, complete with flowers, chocolates, strawberries, champagne, and the works. These children of ours are something to be proud of - a family united. My mind briefly went back to my earlier marriage, which had taken a heavy toll on my life and spirituality. My faith was weak; my heart was tormented. But God often uses our problems to draw us near to Him and places our faith on a solid foundation. He will wipe all the tears from our eyes. Through our sorrow and pain, He will never leave us alone.

It seems the only decision my new husband and I need to make is which church we're going to attend. Neither of our pastors wanted us to leave, but after extensive discussion, John and I decided that I would leave my church. We could always visit my church if we'd like. I believe that spouses should attend the same church. Besides, John works with the young men of his church, and must continue to do so. I love this man, and I would follow him wherever he goes. I never wanted to follow Josh any place because of the way he humiliated me - leaving me unable to trust any man. My Heavenly Father has changed me from the inside out. Now, I can love again, and He has given me a wonderful man.

> **Psalm 9:10:** ***"And they that know thy name will put their trust in thee: for thou Lord, hast not forsaken them that seek thee."***

My husband and I are striving to accomplish remarkable things in the name of the Lord, for He has done wonderful things for us. John is still working extremely hard with the young men of his church, and I am organizing a young women's group that will begin meeting soon. We both have deep and abiding faith. We're trusting God through our faith, we're walking by faith, and we're living every day of our lives by faith. We stop to remember that we cannot do anything on our own - we need the help of our beloved Savior to lead and direct our daily walk.

I found out today that the Lord is adding another blessing to our family. My son, Greg, and his wife, Marcie, are expecting a baby girl or boy. I am so happy. John found out today that there is an opening at his job, and he was offered the position. He will not have to travel for work anymore.

My family and I have so much to be thankful for as we approach Thanksgiving. This will be our first Thanksgiving together as a married couple. Everyone will be coming to dinner at John's and my house, but we don't mind. We look forward to a blessed day as a blended family. Thanksgiving is always a time for family and friends to come together and celebrate, giving thanks. We're in for an exciting time, with a wonderful dinner featuring turkey and all the trimmings. I will make Mama's special sweet potato pie.

We decided that John's daughter, Beth, and her husband, Donald, would host our Christmas celebration. I have always loved the Christmas holiday, and I make sure that we all remember the reason we celebrate this day. Of course, John and I will celebrate with our young people at church. We decided to host a gift exchange and social event, which allowed our guests to dress up, bring a date, and stay off the streets on Christmas Eve. This will be the first time I've done this, but it won't be the last. Our groups are excited and working hard.

Kathy, Doris, and others have been working on our office Christmas party. I am glad they didn't ask me to help because my hands are full working with the young people at church.

When I got home from work, I got a call from Sandra and the only thing I could do was cry. I called her back.

"Girl, why haven't you called? Is everything all right?"

"Everything's wonderful, Susie. I babysit every day with my grandchildren, as well as my daughter's friend's children. I am busy."

"I would say so. How many children are you keeping?"

"My goodness, honey, I have five of them, and one is a newborn. I feel like a new parent all over again."

"Girl, please, do not even go there. We have had our share of that in years past. God bless you for having the courage to attempt that again. I miss you so much. Everyone at work is asking about you. I will have to tell them what you are doing. When are you coming home? I heard that David is still seeing his friend. I hate to think about him being with anybody except you, but it sounds like that is not going to change."

"No, I do not think so, Susie. I hope you and your family had a blessed Thanksgiving."

"Oh, yes, we did. Please tell your daughter Kattie hello for me."

"Yes, I will, and you tell John and the children hello for me. I love you, girl."

"I love you, too, Sandra." I was thrilled to hear from her, so I called John at work to share the news.

Ring, ring.

"Hello, my darling daughter."

"Hi, Mama, what are you doing?"

"My dear, I just had a call from Sandra."

"So, what is she doing these days?"

"You will never guess what she is doing. She's babysitting her grandchildren, plus

Kattie's friend's children, and one is a newborn. But she's happy."

"Mama, I am so glad that you heard from her. When is she coming home?"

"Honey, she said "no way soon, she's not ready."

"Okay, Mama. I just wanted to check on you. I talked to Tommy today. He's doing all right and said to tell you and everyone hello. I'll talk to you later. Love you, Mom."

"I love you, too, my baby."

Sometimes, with all the hustle and bustle of the holiday, we often forget others who are less fortunate than we are. We feel all warm and fuzzy inside and want to give for that one day. We forget the other three hundred and sixty-four days. God wants us to see the needs of our fellow man every day because there is a continuous need in the world. He wants us to have the mind and spirit to lend a helping hand to the sick and shut-in and to people experiencing homelessness.

I am also guilty of neglecting my obligations in that area. We must remember that not all needs are monetary. We can share our spare time, our love, and the blessings we've been given - such as shelter, food, and clothing. We must remember these things as we celebrate the holidays.

Our celebration with the young people's group was a real success - we hope to make this an annual event. We attended late night service, and just like that, the New Year has come and gone. John and I are looking forward to another year of blessings.

"I WILL NEVER TURN BACK"
(Prayer of Thanksgiving)

"Heavenly Father, I praise Your Holy Name because You are so worthy of praise.

You have kept my children and me from all hurt, harm, and danger.

I am so grateful, Heavenly Father, for all You have done in my life.

Lord, You have brought me a long way.

You blessed me to reunite with my brother and other family members.

I have dear friends who are close to my heart.

I thank You, Lord, for my children who were able to stay in their father's life so that he could be a part of his grandchildren's lives.

As I lie here tonight remembering what You said in Your Word that You would give me the desires of my heart, and You have done that.

Heavenly Father, thank You for blessing me with a new husband and extended family. Thank You for fulfilling Your Word through me; my cup runs over.

Lord, You also said in Your Word that You will never leave me nor forsake me.

Continue to bless me spiritually and prosper me,

that I may be a blessing to others in need.

I WILL NEVER TURN BACK!

Thank You, God, for Your Son Jesus, because it is in His Holy and

Righteous Name that I pray. Amen."

As John and I sow seed in the new year, we're trusting God to lead and guide us in His word and wisdom to be good role models for these young people He has entrusted to us. We want to lead by His guidance and not replace Him in their lives. We want God to let us be lowly in at heart and mind, so that they may come to us with any and every capacity of their lives. The scripture says:

Proverbs 22:6: ***Train up a child in the way he should go: and when he is old, he will not depart from it.***

Sometimes, I must catch myself when speaking to these young people because my upbringing was under different rules than those of children today. My parents were extremely strict - there were things that we could not do, places that we could not go, and things we dared not say. We were taught to respect our elders, and that still applies to my life today. I've come to realize that I need to pray over time. John and I are determined, with the Lord's help, to raise these young people to be God-fearing men and women. We are sure going to try.

Today has been a stormy day, washing all the impurities from the earth and from us. I am thankful to Him for sending everything that we need at the right time. We have a new addition to our family. Greg and Marcie have a little daughter, Brandy Kay. Greg Jr. is so happy to have a little sister, and Grandma is happy too.

My sister Leslie called to tell me that she and Bradley are expecting a baby in seven months. I was shouting loudly and praising God. John thought I had lost my mind. They have been trying for such a long time to have a child. Thank you, God - Hallelujah!

We received more good news from John's son, Stanley, who is coming home to join the law firm of a good family friend as a junior partner. God is truly great.

CHAPTER 11
Memorial Day Trip Back Home

Memorial Day is right upon us. I was telling Doris and Kathy that I plan to go back home to Kansas for the holiday. We have been discussing visiting my parents' graves over Memorial Day weekend, and spending time with my Aunt Martha, Uncle Fred, and Aunt Doreen. I have not seen them since Mama died and I am excited about showing off my husband.

Doris said, "Frank and I are going home, too."

Kathy said, "Okay, just leave me here alone for the holiday."

"I'm sorry, Kathy, but do you realize how long it's been since I've gone home?"

"Yes, I know. I'm just kidding."

"We know, honey, but it would be nice if the two of you could get away from here for a day or two."

"Yes, it would," Kathy said. "In fact, Robert wants me to go with him and the kids to see his brother, but I don't want to go because my brother-in-law's wife and I can't get along. We can't ever see eye to eye about anything."

"Well, Kay, can't you put up with her for a few days?"

"I guess I could." Kathy said. "But it will not be easy. I'm telling you that woman drives me crazy."

"Well, honey, if it's that bad, maybe you shouldn't go. Pray about it. I'm sure Robert wants to get you away from everything," Doris said.

"Well, that's not the place for me to get away from things, believe me."

Memorial Day came, and we all did what we planned. My son, daughter, and their children went with us to Kansas - which was a surprise - but it made me incredibly happy. We had a magnificent time. Everyone was thrilled to see my children had grown up and with children of their own. My aunts and uncle were delighted to meet my husband, and my children also got to see their father. He was excited to meet his grandchildren. It was good to visit Mama's and Daddy's graves. I felt bad that I hadn't been back - hopefully, this wouldn't be the last time. John said he loved my part of the country. I was glad someone loved it, because I couldn't wait to leave. I had so many bad memories - which is why it took me so long to come back.

CHAPTER 12

The Loss Of Our Best Friend

We returned home safely, but we received troubling news. Our friend Kathy became ill on their trip and had to be hospitalized. Robert told us that she passed out. The Doctors are still trying to figure out what is wrong with her, running all kinds of tests. I am worried about our friend and pray that it is not serious, and she will be all right. At church on Sunday, we offered prayers for her, and I promised that we would keep her job covered until she returned. Although it has been hard working because we can't stop thinking about her, we will continue to do so. I told John that if she were not better by the weekend, we would go to see her. Friday morning, Robert called to give us an update about his wife. I could tell right away that he was upset.

"What's wrong, Robert? Is Kathy alright?"

"No, Susie, she's not. The doctor said my baby has lung cancer."

"No, no, no, don't tell me that, there must be a mistake, are they sure, Robert?"

"Yes, Susie, I'm sure they have run so many tests and scopes."

"Oh no, Robert, I am so sorry. What can we do?" We will do whatever you need us to do. I will get the house ready for her."

"Oh, no need, Susie, I am taking her straight to the hospital. We'll see you when we arrive. Thank you. I called the kids. You can check on them if you do not mind."

"Of course we will."

"Oh mercy, let me call Doris, John, honey, I just can't believe that our friend is so ill, I just can't."

"Baby, don't cry, everything will be alright, here let me call Doris for you."

"Thanks, baby, I am sick to my stomach, I can't imagine what Robert's going through, and poor Kathy's probably so scared."

"Honey, I talked to Doris, and called the children, and they're okay. I told them to call if they need anything, so maybe we'll go on to work and take the children a pizza or something."

"Yeah, no use worrying our kids so early in the morning."

After Kathy arrived at the hospital, we went to visit her. Oh my, she looked so pale and was having trouble breathing, but she was in good spirits and glad to see us. I had to hold it together for her. Their children were there; they seemed utterly dismayed, along with Robert. Lord, have mercy; he needs your strength. I called Doris, and she and her husband Frank arrived, so we left the room for a while to let them in. I needed to calm down. I've known Kathy for an exceptionally long time, and she is good at hiding her true feelings. My friend won't make it through this. I can feel it; that's why it's so hard to bear. Doris said she felt it too. God, I know that you know best, but it's so hard. Lord, please do not take our friend away from us and her family. Kathy, Doris, and I have been close friends ever since I moved here. If anything were to happen to my girl, nothing would ever be the same for us. Sandra has gone out of state, and we miss her, but we can still talk to her.

Our friend Kathy passed away two days later. My friend fought hard to stay for her family and friends. She is now resting in the loving arms of Jesus. I will take comfort knowing that, but it hurts. Most importantly, she is leaving behind a loving husband and two wonderful children who need her at this time in their lives, especially her daughter, Kim, and son, Bobby. But he has his father to shape him; however, he is devastated right now.

We met Kathy's two sisters and her brother: they are so much like Kathy. I pray that they will step up and help Robert with the children; if not, he has Kathy's friends and Pastor Berry for support. All this happens so quickly during the Memorial Day weekend. Kathy's service was on Saturday; everything was lovely. Sad, but Robert gave her a beautiful homegoing. Doris and I were flower bearers; John, Frank, and other friends were casket bearers. Reverend Berry gave the eulogy, and my mind wandered back to the day when no one knew anything about cancer or how to treat it. People just died, and it was called natural causes. It also holds true for dementia. They would say that the person lost their mind.

My friend's death has taken its toll on me. I have been depressed, not eating or sleeping, not wanting to go to work because Kathy would not be there. I have neglected the young women's group. John's worried about me; he is doing everything to snap me out of it. I regret that I was unable to help Robert with the children when I couldn't help myself. I realized that they were moving on with their lives better than Doris and me, so I had to apologize to Robert and the children for my weakness. However, they understood and thanked me for the love I had for Kathy. I truly loved her like a sister and always will.

I also apologize to my husband for being such a burden to him. Even a good man gets tired of a lost cause, I thought that was what I had become. You know, a woman could lose her man to someone else who shows him that he's needed and not just a mop to clean up the spills of his wife's breakdown. Oh Lord, do not let me lose John that way, I would have to be locked up for sure, he's the best thing in my life right now, I can't go back to what I was, lost and lonely, afraid to live or love. John has given me everything; he is the kind of man any woman would kill to have. I'm not sure why I'm thinking this way; he hasn't given me any indication that he feels the same. Lord forbid, I'm thankful to have had a dear friend like Kathy, but the Lord has taken her to a better place. And I need to accept that and move on with my life.

CHAPTER 13
The Lost Of Our Oldest Grandson

The Fourth of July is approaching quickly, and we haven't planned anything special. We will have a barbecue with the family. John and I agreed to take all our grandchildren in for an overnight stay. We have never kept them all at once, but we are looking forward to it. We went out and bought all these goodies that they love, yes, we planned to spoil them rotten. I have been trying to keep myself busy to avoid constantly thinking about Kathy, but I've come to realize that time heals all wounds.

The grandchildren wanted to go swimming, so we loaded them all into the SUV and headed to the pool. They were so happy and excited. Our grandson, Greg Jr., is a good swimmer, but the rest of the grandchildren are not.

We had to keep a close eye on them when they were in the pool, and we thought we were, but John's grandson, Raymond, somehow slipped away and got into the pool. Greg Jr. came running to us screaming,

"Grandpa, Grandma, Raymond went under the water and did not come up! The lifeguards pulled him out, and he was not breathing."

"Oh Heavenly Father, please, don't let this happen," I screamed.

John ran to him as fast as he could. I told Greg Jr. to keep an eye on the others. When we got to Raymond, his little body was limp, and they were trying to revive him. John cried out,

"Is he all right? Please, please do not let my grandson die, oh God, do not let him die." He kept saying over and over, do not let him die. They took him to the hospital; John went with him; I stayed with the other children. I called Beth and Donald to tell them what happened. My daughter Valerie took the other children to her house, and my son Greg took me to the hospital.

My husband was a complete mess, understandably, so Donald was trying to comfort Beth. Oh Lord, I pray, what are we going to say to them? I thought to myself, we should not have taken them to the pool, just the two of us trying to keep an eye on them all. I was holding John in my arms, which is all I could do for him at that moment. I had never seen him so upset. Then they came out to tell us that they had done all they could to save him. Everyone broke down in tears. Beth was screaming,

'No, no!' John pushed me away and went to his daughter. He had just lost his only grandson, and what made it even worse, it was on our watch. We should have been watching him better; I kept thinking. Lord, I pray that Beth and Donald will find it in their broken hearts to forgive us one day, but how can they, when we cannot forgive ourselves?

My daughter and my son went over to comfort Beth and Donald, but when I went over to say something, Beth began to scream at me, "How could you and Daddy let my baby drown? How could you?

"I said, honey, I'm sorry it was an accident."

"Then John said, baby, you know how Raymond likes to run off, he just sneaked away from us and got into the pool without our knowledge, I would have given my life for that boy, you know that I'm sorry, baby."

He took her in his arms, and they wept together. All I could do was pray and ask the Lord to intercede and give us the strength to accept this. Raymond was always running off somewhere. It was hard for Beth to keep track of him; the older he got, the worse he became. I hate that something like this happened the first time we had our grandchildren over. I am so grateful that the rest of them are all right.

As John and I drove home, neither one of us said a word to each other. I'm unsure how this will affect our marriage, given all the recent challenges that have strained our relationship, starting with Kathy and now including our grandson.

> ***"Therefore humble yourself therefore under the mighty hands of God, that He may exalt you in due time." 1 Peter 5:6***

We didn't think much about the fourth weekend, except for a tragic event in the family. Our grandchildren were crying, unable to understand what had happened to Raymond. Their parents were trying to explain the accident, but there is just no explanation; only God knows. I asked John if there was anything I could do for him. He said,

"No, baby, there's nothing you can do."

"Honey, you need to eat. Can I get you a salad or a sandwich?"

"Yes, that sounds good. I am not hungry, but I need to eat." He told me.

"Alright, maybe we can lie down after we eat and take a nap." Because my body felt drained, and I knew he was too.

Ring, ring, "hello."

"Hi, Mama, how are you and John doing?"

"Hi Honey, we're doing alright as well as can be expected. I'm getting ready to fix something to eat."

"Have you heard from Beth and Donald yet?"

"No, Mom, I was wondering if you all had heard from them."

"No, we have not. John will call them later, and I will let you know."

"Ok, mama, let me know if I can do anything for them."

"I will, baby, love you."

Saturday morning was Raymond's funeral service. It was sad that no one could contain themselves; my heart went out to Beth and Donald. John became so upset that his sons, Stanley and Paul, and I had to take him out of the service. Reverend Falconers preached a sermon that was befitting the occasion for our little Raymond. John's brother had to talk to him because he could see that he was blaming himself for what happened. We couldn't have that because he'd never be able to forgive himself or allow his daughter to heal. She already felt it was our fault anyway. Oh my, I'd do anything to prevent this from being the case, but all we can do is pray that she will someday overcome this with God's help; she will.

Everybody went back to work on Monday, except Beth and Donald, who understandably needed to take the time off. The following Sunday, after church, John and I stopped by to check on them. Donald was noticeably quiet, but he did talk to us. Beth did not say anything; she just ran upstairs. Donald said she has not been out of the house since the funeral; she barely gets out of bed, will not eat, and is not sleeping.

"I'm going upstairs to talk to her," John said. But when he got upstairs, I could hear her screaming at him to get out and leave me alone. He told her that he would not leave her alone. Raymond is gone, baby, we are all hurting, but you need to move on. Visit Doctor Burns so he can prescribe something to help you rest.

"I do not need a doctor, daddy, I need my baby, I need my baby, she cried.

"I will not let you do this to yourself, Honey. What about your husband? He is worried about you, we all are," John told her.

She came running downstairs, John running after her. When she looked at me, she said, "It is your fault that my baby is gone. You should not have taken them to the pool. You and Daddy knew you couldn't watch all those children."

"Alright, alright, now that's enough. I know you're hurting, but you know it's no one's fault. Things happen; you know we never meant for this to happen. We just wanted the kids to enjoy themselves, and we did everything humanly possible to keep our grandchildren safe. Beth, my darling girl, you need to apologize to my wife." John told her.

"I'm sorry, Mama Susie", as we wept in each other's arms.

"Beth, my darling, I love you so much. I know that you're in pain, and I know that you didn't mean anything you said. But you and Donald must let the rest of the family be here for you, lean on us to get through this hurt, together as a family, alright, baby?"

"Ok, Mama Susie, we will do that," Donald said.

My son Greg and wife Marcie called while we were there and invited all of us over for Sunday dinner. Beth did not want to go, but Donald said, tell them we will be there.

"Honey, you need to get out of this house, get some fresh air. We're just going to Greg and Marcie's house; you'll be fine."

"Ok, ok, I'll go," Beth said."

"Oh yes, Beth and Donald, I almost forgot to tell you that Pastor Falconer said he'd be stopping by very soon to check on you all, but he'll call first."

We are all barely functioning, even our grandchildren, and our marriages have all been affected. John needs some time to himself. I keep praying that things will get better. He spends most of his spare time with his daughter, rather than with me lately. I don't want to come across as envious of my stepdaughter, but I need my husband. I asked him if I had done something to upset him. Of course, he said no. Usually, he would reassure me with a hug or a kiss, but this time he just said no, and that was that. I asked him if he would like to go for a walk. He went, at least his body did, but his mind was elsewhere. What can I do to get him out of this mood? I realize he lost his only grandson. I want to help him get through it if he lets me in.

CHAPTER 14
Affected All Our Relationships

It has been months since we lost Raymond, but it seems like yesterday. I decided to visit my sister in California for a week, hoping that when I return, John would be in a better frame of mind. I told Leslie how he was acting. She asked, "Well, Susie, are you sure that he's not blaming you somehow for the accident?"

"Oh no, Les I hope not. Does he blame me? I gasp, like Beth does? I insisted on taking the children swimming. I will certainly find out when I get back."

Leslie and I had a lovely short visit, but I had not seen her baby. She is so beautiful, and Les is a good mom. Bradley is a proud papa; they are doing fine. We spoke with my brother Herbert while I was there. He and his family were doing all right. He told me just to be patient with John; his daughter lost her only child, and he lost his only grandson. He needs a little time. "Thanks, Herbert, I'll do that."

Oh, mercy, my time was up with my visit to Leslie and Bradley; I was looking forward to seeing my husband when I got home. Friends from church told me that Grace, a woman who was hot for my husband before he and I began dating, had been all up in his face while I was gone. Please, Lord, please do not let my husband be slipping away from me. I love him so much; he is a good man, and I do not believe he would do anything like that to me. Doris also told me that she saw them at the Burger Barn on Friday before I got back. I need to have a heart-to-heart with my husband. I never in a million years thought he would do anything like that, knowing my history with cheating men.

On Sunday, after church, I made a nice dinner for the two of us, featuring his favorites. Later, we had a long talk about what was happening between us. I flat-out asked him.

"Nothing is going on, Honey. I love you." He told me.

"So, tell me then, what's up with Grace and you?"

"Baby, don't be ridiculous; she's just a friend." He told me.

"Well, that is the way it starts, and why did she become your friend while I was out of town, John? I no longer understand what's going on with you. You're moody, quiet, and barely talk to me? Ever since Raymond's accident, you have been distant toward me, John. I love you so much, do not do this to me, please."

"Honey, why are you talking like this? Nothing's wrong, we're good?"

"You haven't even been meeting with the young men's group; they keep asking and calling to see if there's going to be a meeting, but you're always at Beth's house. Are you ever going back to teaching?"

"They're worried about you; baby, talk to me, let me help."

"You can't help me, Susie, just leave me alone."

"Oh no, you want me to leave you alone." I ran upstairs crying. He didn't even come after me. I stayed in our bedroom all night. He slept on the sofa and left early for work before I got up.

I called my friend Doris, crying, all upset.

"What's wrong, Susie? Please tell me what's going on." I was so upset that I didn't even go to work. And went to talk to our Pastor.

"What's happening with John, Reverend Falconer? Has he mentioned anything to you?"

"No, baby, he hasn't said anything to me. What's wrong?"

"That's the problem, Pastor. I don't know, he's been acting strange ever since Raymond died. I can't reach him; he doesn't talk to me, and when I ask him, he says nothing or responds with, "Leave me alone."

"Don't you worry, child. I'll talk to him. I'll get to the bottom of this. I know he loves you. He probably needs a little more time to process the loss of his grandchild, and he's feeling partly responsible."

The Pastor did call John, and John got angry because I had gone to our Pastor; he said, "How dare you run to our Pastor with our problems?'

"I went to him because you won't talk to me. Maybe if we got away from here for a while and work things out."

"I need to stay here with Beth; she needs me."

"John, she has a husband, he'll take care of her; we need to work on us."

"Susie, if you lost one of your grandchildren, you'd be feeling the same way. I find myself questioning God; that's how bad it is. You know that's not like me."

"So just stop. Susie, you're working my nerves."

I went upstairs, packed a bag, and stayed with my daughter, Valerie. Since he wants to be alone, I thought, be alone.

"And whatsoever ye do in word or deed, do all in the name of the Lord Jesus, giving thanks to God and the Father by him." Colossians 3:17

John's brother called and told me that he had spoken to John, and John told him that you're staying with Valerie.

"Well, Benjamin, he wanted to be alone."

"Susie, what in the world is going on with you two?"

"All I can tell you is that ever since Raymond's death, John has been distance toward me like he thinks I'm responsible for Raymond's death, and when he does say anything to me it's mean and sometimes harsh, so I just left to give him his space and more time to grieve, evidently that's what he needs, this is the second time I've left. I hope and pray that this isn't the end of us. Ben he's even been hanging out with this woman he dated before he met me. I don't know what's up with that."

"Did you ask him?" Ben asked.

"I did, he said nothing's going on, and that I can't believe everything I hear. Well, I thought I'd never have to worry about anything like this. I'm tired of people telling me to give him time. He's had time; if we take any more time, this marriage will be over, Ben."

"Susie, we'll be down there in a week. I'll get to the bottom of this."

"Ok, but don't dare tell him that you talked to me about this, or I asked you to come, which I didn't."

When I got to work, Doris was all over me.

"What's happening to you and John, Susie? Just talk to me?" She asked me.

"Doris, there's nothing to talk about; my husband is done with me."

"Oh girl, you don't mean that, he loves you."

"He did love me, and I promised myself that never again would I let any man hurt me."

"Do you think this situation is happening because of Grace?"

"No, Doris, I just think it's the fact that he is still hurting over Raymond; he wasn't even at church on Sunday. It felt strange not having him sitting there beside me."

Pastor asks. "Where is your husband? I have been trying to reach him all week, but he hasn't returned my calls. I will keep trying and praying for him, baby, and you do the same."

"I want to stop praying, Pastor. He will work it out in time. And deal with whatever is troubling him. In the meantime, I will continue to do my work with my girls and attend church, praising God. I will wait for Him as long as I can, and God sees fit. No one in our family understands what is going on; how can I explain it when I don't know myself?"

Sunday was a good day. Reverend Falconer preached a wonderful sermon. He talked about "Giving God the Glory".

"Whether therefore ye eat, or drink, or whatsoever ye do, do all to the glory of God." 1 Corinthians 10:31.

My son took us all out to dinner on Sunday: Valerie, Michael, the kids, and me. I found myself missing John because that was something we did every Sunday; I just wanted to go over there and shake him. On Thursday evening, I met with my girls, and they began asking questions about Brother Barter. I knew eventually they would. Brother Barter is going through a great deal right now; girls, please keep him in your prayers. One of them said, "We heard that you were not living with him; you were staying with your daughter."

"Yes, that's right, Honey. I am giving Brother Barter the time he needs to get over his grandson's death."

"Well, Sister Barter, I know that the two of you still love each other; you can't stop loving each other. This sucks."

"Yes, baby, we do still love each other, and that's what makes it so hard, but let's get to our lesson for tonight, alright?"

It's now the end of October, and the weather is getting a little cooler outside. The trees are beginning to change. I still take my daily walks in the park, hoping to run into John, but I haven't seen him yet. I keep thinking maybe tomorrow.

CHAPTER 15

Coming Together For The Holiday's

Friday after work, I took my grandchildren to the park. As I was running around playing with them, I looked up and there stood John. He said, "Hi, beautiful, just like you were when we first met." I ran to him, and we embraced. The children ran to him, saying,

"Grandpa, Grandpa, we missed you."

"I missed you all, too, he said. I'm sorry, baby. I'm so, so sorry. I've been such a fool. Please forgive me. I thought I'd lost you."

"No, John, you'll never lose me. I miss you so much."

"Will you have dinner with me so we can talk about how stupid I've been?"

"Yes, I'll come home to change after I drop the children off."

The children ran home to tell Valerie what happened. They said, 'Mama, Mama, we saw Grandpa at the park.' Alright, get cleaned up for dinner. "Oh, Mama, I knew that John still loved you; that's wonderful."

"I'm having dinner with John."

"Okay Mama."

"Please don't wait for me," we laughed.

John and I had a nice dinner. We talked. He told me that when his brother came for a visit, we talked for a long time. Then we prayed together. He said the first time this happened to me was when Mama died, but it was nothing like this. I had a hard time dealing with my grandson's death. My brother told me to get a grip, this isn't the first time you'll lose someone you love, and it won't be the last. Things like this will happen in our lives, John, but you grieve your loss and then move on. He said Man, you're about to lose the best thing in your life since your children's mother died. You'd better pray that it's not too late for you and Susie.

"Tell me it's not too late."

"John, I've never seen you act like this, and it scared me."

"Susie, honey, he's right, you're good for me, we're good for each other. I even began to turn away from God, and that's when I started to feel depression settling in. How could I ever turn away from God? I've been fasting and praying, asking God to forgive me. And I need to apologize to those young men for the way I've neglected them."

> **"A merry heart maketh a cheerful countenance: but by sorrow of the heart the spirit is broken." Proverbs 15:13**

Thanksgiving is coming up, and believe me, we have a lot to be thankful for this year. As we plan our celebration, we also want to find a way to come together in honor of Raymond. Christmas was His favorite holiday. We decided that everyone would buy Raymond a gift since he enjoys receiving them. On Christmas Eve, we selected two families from our church and presented them with the gifts. Beth and Donald thought that was an exceptionally clever idea, and

Raymond would be pleased. On Thanksgiving Day, after our prayer for dinner, Beth and Donald announced that they were expecting a child. We were all crying with excitement, hugging each other. John was so excited that he could not contain himself; he said,

"I am going to be a grandpa again."

I said, "Yes, you are, yes, you are. God is good - He keeps on blessing this family."

John's son called to tell his dad that he had made a full partnership in his firm. My son, Thomas, is engaged and will be bringing his fiancée to meet the family for Christmas. Praise God, my sister Leslie, Bradley, and the baby would be here for the Christmas day celebration. Oh, Hallelujah, we are going to have a wonderful time, with a whole house full and children running all over the place.

On Sunday at Church, John and I stood before the congregation to publicly give God praise and ask not only Him but the whole church to forgive our actions. We almost allowed a tragedy to destroy our faith in Him, and it nearly broke our family apart. But praise be to the all-knowing Heavenly Father, He saw the best in us. He recognized the love that we have for Him as well as for each other and brought us back from the edge. Thank you for keeping us in your prayers during the loss of our grandson. We are ready to get back to work for the Lord. Pastor Falconer asked that the church continue in prayer for us. He said, I know that God brought these two together and they're a God-fearing couple. He still has great things in store for them. We love you, and God loves you too.

After Christmas, we were all so tired that we skipped New Year's, except for the New Year's Eve service at church, and we had a wonderful time. Then it was time for everyone to go back to work, which was really depressing. Doris said that she and her family also had a great holiday together. I did manage to talk to Robbert,

Kathy's husband, and her children. This was their first holiday without their mom. He said it was difficult, but the children did all right. He also told me that he had begun to date, nothing serious. I told him that I understood. Kathy would want you to do that. Kathy's replacement at work learned Kathy's job quickly. Things have moved on. You know the saying, "I am learning to accept the things I cannot change and embrace the things that I can."

It is reassuring to have family and friends. I found out this week that Casey's boyfriend is still hanging around. Ms. Cox, Casey's mom, said that Casey had told him to leave her alone, but he passes by their house many times a day. I know that they are frightened. When they called the police, of course, it's not a crime to drive down a street, but that's harassment; I'm worried about them. John has already warned me not to do anything crazy, but when someone is in trouble, I want to help; sometimes, all I can do is pray. I spoke with John's son, Paul, the attorney, to see if anything could be done, but he reiterated the police's stance. But of course, Paul had to tell John that I was asking questions concerning the situation. I wanted to keep John out of it. That night, he put me on notice,

"Stay out of it, honey," he said.

"But John, you don't understand, Casey's one of my young ladies, you know that her mom is a single parent trying to care for three children by herself, that's tough enough as it is."

"I understand all that, honey, what do you think you can do, except get yourself hurt?" he said.

"But baby, I was thinking that maybe we could help them find a decent place to stay, we could do that, couldn't we?"

"Oh, now you are getting into that woman's personal stuff, and you do not know that much about her; maybe she does not want to move. Is Casey enticing this young man? Do you know how she really feels? about him?"

"Oh, please, how can she feel anything for him, for he's a gangster and a drug dealer?" "Listen to yourself, that is the very reason we should stay clear of this baby; it could get dangerous. We have already had a tragedy in this family, and we do not want another."

"I knew you'd bring that up again. God has been good to us, and He continues to bless our family. I just wanted to reach out to someone else."

"It seems like no matter what I say, you're still going to get involved in this mess. Well, Sue, don't expect me to help you get yourself hurt."

CHAPTER 16
Danger Ahead

I talked to my son Greg about his help. He said,

"Mama, John's right. You should be careful about what you get yourself involved in. You know John's still a little sensitive about his family's safety. I feel bad for the young lady, but I'm not sure what you can do. Mamma, this young lady has got herself mixed up with bad people, and for the safety of our family, please leave it alone. I do not want anything to happen to you."

I called Casey's mom and invited them over for lunch. We talked about what was going on with this young man and where she met him. Mrs. Barter, I met him through a girl from school. We went out a couple of times, usually with his friends.

"Casey, honey, what do you do?"

"We just sit around listening to music, smoking weed, and drinking."

"Oh, honey, how could you get yourself mixed up with a gang member?"

"It wasn't my intention, but Donna invited me to a party one night and introduced me to Mark. He seemed nice at first, then he began acting like he had claims on me. He wanted me to smoke with him, but when I told him that I didn't want to, he got very angry. I stopped hanging out with him, that is when he threatened me."

"Oh my, how did he threaten you, with what?"

"My family, he said, 'I know where you live and I know where your little brother hangs out, he said you're my woman for life.' "He is crazy, Mrs. Barter. Now he is driving by my house. I am afraid, what can I do?" She sobs.

"I don't know, honey, we'll figure something out." We held hands and prayed.

I know this is not going to end well. I sighed. Maybe my family's right; I shouldn't get involved, but I can't sit around and do nothing. The child's afraid. What can I do? My son-in-law is a police officer, and he has been on the force for a long time. Maybe I'll talk to him. I know my daughter will be upset with me, but she'll get over it. I called Michael and asked him what we could do. Well, Mom, he said, about what everyone else has told you, no crime has been committed, but I will put extra police officers on her street. I called Jeanette and told her what Michael said. Until they do something, there is nothing they can do. I know that it is a shame that someone must get hurt, killed, or beaten before the law can intervene. Lord, be merciful and watch over our families.

I told my husband what I had found out, he sympathizes with the family, but he is still telling me to stay out of it and not to get involved.

"But John, honey, I just can't, I have to find some way to help."

"Oh my goodness, woman, why can't you ever listen to reason? I am trying to protect the woman that I love, please let me do that? For my sake, yours, and our family, you need to stop this. You have been asking too many questions. How long do you think it will be before this gang comes after someone you love? You know that the police are not going to do anything until somebody gets hurt or killed. Please, baby, do not let it be you; we cannot protect you twenty-four-seven."

Sunday at church, I got up and addressed the congregation about this problem, asking them to pray for the well-being of our young people. We need to keep them safe from the likes of all this violence, drugs, and threats to our teens and young adults. Be aware of who they spend time with, including their friends and family. It is already in our schools, now it is trying to invade our churches. God, please bless our children.

After church, Doris stopped by, and we talked about it.

"Maybe you can talk some sense into my wife Doris. She insists on ridding the state of gang violence," John said. I know that I cannot see God, but He is with me in spirit, so I rely on Him to always be with me.

> **Jesus said, "My sheep hear my voice, and I know them, and they follow me:**
>
> **And I give unto them eternal life; and they shall never perish, neither shall any man pluck them out of my hand."** ***John 10:27-28.***

I am not trying to go against my husband. I love him, and I know that he loves me, and he only wants to keep me safe. I want to help this young lady who is in my women's group as best as I can. John knows he would do the same thing if one of his young men were in trouble, I know he would. We both dedicated our lives to this. I pray that our Deacons from our church would sit down and talk to Mark. I know that is asking too much, but God is able, and we know we can do all things through Him.

Wednesday night, instead of regular Bible study, the Pastor allowed us to have a special prayer service and a guest speaker. We also invited other churches in the city to come and bring their youth groups. We asked Casey to invite Mark and his boys. Praise God, they agreed to meet with us. We had Deacons, Pastors, and group leaders in attendance. Our guest speaker was Mr. Daryl Coleman from the city, who specializes in local gang violence. Mark showed up with his boys. Thank God they were quiet and well-mannered; they sat and listened to everything. After Mr. Coleman spoke, our Pastor, Reverend Falconer, spoke to the groups.

Pastor said, "Young men and women, can any of you tell us why you are wasting your life on junk?" Do any of you know anything about your Lord and Savior? Would you like to know Him? Do you know why He died for you? He did not give His life for you to take someone else's. No, I do not believe that he did. God is your Savior because He saved us all from ourselves. Pastor Falconer told us. So young people tell me, "Why are you dishonoring God our Savior with this junk? He gave His life to rid the world of sin. He took all our sins up on Hin self so that we could live free from sin, yet you're living a life that's not pleasing to Him, dishonoring His Almighty name; by hurting, hating, destroying what God has entrusted to you. You are to worship Him in spirit and truth. Stop defying your bodies with junk. This body of yours belongs to God, so stop dishonoring His body with junk."

Have you noticed that no one wants to be around you because you are spreading your junk to little children, and God loves little children. Violating young women, causing fear, destroying homes and neighborhoods, even your own. Do these things make you feel good, or make you feel like a real man, or just a bully? Please think about what I have said. Here's your chance to let God come into your life, right here, right now. He can make you brand new, say God, here I am. I want to live for you, I want to work for you. I want you to come into my heart right now. Say, "God, here I am". He's waiting with open arms; He'll wipe all these bad things away, just come to Him with a sincere heart because He loves you. Think about it right now, young people, give me your hand and give God your heart. All we can do is ask; the rest is up to you, but we will continue to pray for you. God bless you. One other thing I would like to know, Pastor Falconer asked, "Where are your parents?" What do they think of the life you have chosen for yourselves? I bet they are not pleased."

Mark stood up,

"Uh, yes, Pastor Sir. We have heard everything that you all said, and we will think about it. Pastor Sir, if you do not mind, thank you for the invitation."

Pastor said, "Thank you for coming. We hope that you will come again. Our doors are always open."

They got up and left. Mark blew a kiss at Casey, which embarrassed her.

"Saints don't stop praying, and thanks to our special guest and all the churches that came out tonight, Pastor Falconer said, let's pray and be dismissed."

On our drive home, John said, he felt optimistic about the outcome of tonight's meeting, at least they came.

"Yes, honey, so did I. I'm glad they weren't disrespectful; it seems as though Mark is their leader. I would like to know who their parents are. Did you see Michael there?"

"Yes, I'm glad he came." I thought about these young men as I prayed for their safety. I felt like a heavy burden was weighing on my heart, and I couldn't explain it. John had to work today, so I finished my housework, then I went over to visit Doris for a while, and I also went to see my boys. I thanked God for my boys. They truly are a blessing to me and not a headache. The same holds true for my daughter; not of my own doing, I owe it all to my Heavenly Father.

> **"Truly the light is sweet, and a pleasant thing it is for the eyes to behold the sun: But if a man live many years, and rejoice in them all; yet let him remember the days of darkness; for they shall be many. All that cometh is vanity. Rejoice, O young man, in thy youth; and let thy heart cheer thee in the days of thy youth, and walk in the ways of thine heart, and in the sight of thine eyes: but know thou, that for all these things God will bring thee into judgment." Ecclesiastes 11:7-9**

The weekend has flown by so fast, where has the time gone? I thought to myself, I've got to go back to work tomorrow. There was more work than usual to do. Doris and I did not get a chance to talk very much. The young lady who replaced Kathy is doing an exceptional job; I invited her to come to our church, and she said that she would love to. Casey said she is still talking to Mark, and he will not give up the gang life. I pray for him all the time, not only for him but also for all young men and women. I pray that they will turn their lives around before it is too late and seek God. He is not hard to find. We only call on the Lord when we feel there is no other alternative. He is a loving God, and sometimes He allows us to get ourselves in deep trouble. Yet, God loves us so much that He takes us back into His loving care, which is just how good and compassionate He is.

My sister-in-law called to tell me that she had to take my brother Herbert to the hospital this morning. She said, Susie, can you get here quickly? He is not doing well. I almost dropped the phone. I called John, and he booked us a flight. We left. As soon as I got there, I went in to see my brother. He was barely conscious. He said, "You are here!" I told him I got here as fast as I could.

"You are going to be fine. Just rest. I am not going any place. I love you."

He said, "Sis, I don't think I am going to beat this one."

"Oh, honey, don't even think that way. I prayed, "Lord, please don't take my brother, please let him come through this, please God." I stayed with him as long as the nurse allowed Christian, and I would not leave him. John insisted that we leave, get a shower, and have something to eat. They told us that he needed to rest. So, go home, and we will call you if there is any change. I could not sleep, so my husband slipped something in my tea, and I slept the rest of the night.

When I woke up, I wanted to call the hospital right away, but Christine had already called, and there was no change. We went back to the hospital, and Christine just sat there holding his hand and praying. Then he took a turn for the worse, and they kicked us out of the room. I lost my sweet brother that night. My sister Leslie and Bradley did not make it in time to say goodbye. I felt so bad for Christine and their children. It was so sad, and my poor sister was having a tough time because she did not get there in time. I was a mess, but John and I were trying to comfort everyone else.

CHAPTER 17
My Brother Herbert Passed

"The Lord is my light and my salvation; whom shall I fear? The Lord is the strength of my life; of whom shall I be afraid?" Psalm 27:1

Planning my brother's funeral was a task that no one was looking forward to doing. We planned a beautiful home-going service for Herbert. There were a lot of people in attendance. My children's visit made me feel good and was a blessing for Christine, my nieces, and nephews. Christine was holding up surprisingly well until we were about to leave. Then she broke down, and Les and I followed suit. Bradley and John had to drag us into the car. I hated leaving them, but we had to go. When I got home, I did not want to go back to work. John tried to get me to quit. I said,

"What will I do all day sitting around here feeling sorry for myself? No thanks." I have been in Constant communication with Christence and the kids, as well as Leslie. They are hanging in there, doing their best to move on with their lives, but they miss her husband and the children's father. It is always good to have your church family to lean on when your biological family cannot be there.

"But let patience have her perfect work, that ye may be perfect and entire, wanting nothing." James 1:4

I finally went back to work, catching up on all the gossip. Kathy's replacement is fitting in well and becoming one of the girls. Before I came back, I got a call from Sandra. She called when she heard about my brother's passing. She mentioned that my sweet daughter had called her, and she's still babysitting for her daughter. Some of my grandchildren are now old enough to attend school, but she enrolled more children to replace them. She's becoming a regular daycare provider. Sandra's moving on with her life after getting a divorce from Robert.

I am still teaching my young ladies at church, but I have also taken up a hobby. My neighbor is teaching me to crochet. It is so fun. I'm excited to teach my granddaughters someday. When the weather gets warmer, John and I plan to work in the yard. I want to plant rose bushes. Everyone is doing all right. I haven't gotten any sad news, thank God. I need to check on my family in Kansas. So much has been going on that I have not had time to tell them about Herbert's passing. I know Aunt Sarah hasn't been feeling well, so I hope she is okay since I haven't heard anything.

Work's going well, Janet. Kathy's replacement has started spending time with us. She's a lot of fun to be around, although I miss Kathy terribly. But all we can do is take one day at a time and count our blessings for every day that God has blessed us with.

Sunday, Pastor Falconer preached a dynamite sermon. I do not know what got into him; people were jumping and shouting all over the place. I could not stay in my seat, nor could John. He preached from

> ***John 1:14, "And the Word was made flesh, and dwelt among us, (and we beheld his glory, the glory as of the only begotten of the Father,) full of grace and truth."***

CHAPTER 18

First Visit To The Senior Center

Wednesday evening at our young ladies meeting, I asked them if they knew of any seniors with whom we could do activities, such as visit, read some scriptures, have a prayer, or anything else that they might need us to do for them.

"With the warmer weather, we can now get out into the community to help those in need. Please think about it and bring the names and addresses to our next meeting, okay, ladies?" "Today I have a treat for you all after bible study, I'm going to take you to get smoothies or ice cream, whatever you want."

"Yes, all right," they screamed.

"I just wanted you to know how much I appreciate all of you. You're the greatest bunch of young ladies, very respectful, and I love you."

"How excellent is thy lovingkindness, O God! therefore the children of men put their trust under the shadow of thy wings." Psalm 36:7.

We had two separate meetings, during which we invited the young lady's mothers. I began by telling the girls a little about how I grew up. As a young lady, I was not allowed to be out after dark alone. Not even playing in my front yard could I have a boyfriend. Oh, I might have a crush on a certain young boy, but only God and I knew about it. They all giggled. Sometimes I wondered how I managed to get married, given how strict my parents were. But regardless of how strict they were, we never, never talked back to them or our elders. Our neighbors were like our parents, and if we did something irresponsible, they were allowed to chastise us when our own parents weren't around. Then if they told our parents, we'd be in trouble. So, we had to be good all the time, because we didn't know who was watching or listening.

My brother, sister, and I did very well in school and were actively involved in our church, which was necessary. We discovered that studying God's word not only strengthened our character but also kept us on the right track. Also, studying made us want to be good human beings and strive to do what was pleasing to Him. So, girls, listen to your parents. They are merely telling you what's right. As you all become young women, remember that your wedding night should be special. If something does not feel right, then it is not. Do not turn away from your goal in life. When you are all grown up and have children of your own, remember what your parents taught you. I thank God for my mother. Yes, she was old school, and there were some things with which I disagreed. One of which was waiting on her husband, my dad, hand and foot - they all giggle - or staying with a man if he is mistreating you or your children, which is a big no-no. I loved you all, and I want to see you all become wives, mothers, and grandparents. Never be afraid to ask questions, whether it's your mother, your Pastor, or someone you trust.

When we met with the mothers, Casey's mother told us that Casey was doing great. I am proud of you all. We are a family united by God. Do not let a little Jack Rabbit sweet-talk you into losing yourself before you are ready - ha, ha, ha - the girls all laughed.

"Things are much different than they were when your mother and I were young, right, mothers? We didn't have much to discuss outside of church or school. Now there are computers with internet, cell phones, e-mails, and drugs. You even have your own cars."

Some of the mothers who attended also addressed the girls. Casey and her mom, Jeanett, became my helpers. I really appreciated that. At the next meeting, we hope to have a speaker come and talk to them about etiquette. They will enjoy learning how to act appropriately as young ladies. This weekend will be our Christmas social. We will be decorating all week. John and I are so proud of them all. Last Sunday after Church, they met briefly to vote on a theme food and refreshment.

CHAPTER 19
Growing Pains

Our Christmas social turned out beautifully. Everyone had an exciting time. Afterward, John and I went home to join our family gathering. We all stayed up half the night celebrating, although we were tired, but a good tired. It was so good to have everyone there. We met Thomas's fiancée. She was a lovely young woman named Barbara. He met her in college. Everyone was there: my son Gregg, his wife Marcie, Gregg Jr., and baby Brandy. Both of John's sons were present. Paul brought his girlfriend Linda, Stanley's wife, and two sons, Stanley Jr. and Frankie, of course, his daughter Beth, and her husband Donald, and their baby boy Ryan. We had a house full of children running everywhere. Calls came in from all over; it was Christmas to remember.

> **"Now when Jesus was born in Bethlehem of Judaea in the days of Herod the king, behold, there came wise men from the east to Jerusalem, saying, Where is he that is born King of the Jews? for we have seen his star in the east, and are come to worship him." Matthew 2:1-2**

On Friday evening, one of our girls in my group, Mother Jeanett, called me. She said her daughter, Casey, had gone to Brooklyn to meet her boyfriend. Ms. Cox, a single mother as I previously mentioned, wanted me to go with her to find her daughter. Well, I was willing to help, not thinking that it might be dangerous. Two women were going over there alone when it began to get dark, and we had not found Casey. When we were about to give up, we saw her with other young people. Ms. Cox called out to her daughter to come home with her; she came over to the car.

"What in the world are you doing over here this late? Your mother has been so worried about you. Come on, and go home." I told her.

"I'm not ready to go home, Mrs. Barter."

"Girl, don't let me have to get out and drag you into this car," Casey told her mom.

"I'll be there later, okay?"

"Mark said What are you two old ladies doing over here, or are you lost? You heard her say she is not ready to go home? Now get out of here."

"Ms. Cox said Please, Casey, let's go home and talk about this."

"Just go home, mama."

I grabbed my cell phone from my purse to call the police or John, but Mark snatched it out of my hand and told us to get lost.

"Please, can I have my phone back? I asked.

"No, now get lost before something else happens to you."

I was so afraid. We lost our directions, and I hadn't been paying attention. We were on the freeway with no phone to call anyone. We drove around for a while until we found a service station, got directions to the freeway, and called John from there. He was upset with me, as I knew he would be. He said,

"Stay right where you are, I am coming to get you."

My husband was so angry that he wanted to find Mark and bring Casey home, but Ms. Cox and I talked him out of it. Oh my, I have not heard the last of this. I thought.

He started, "Why didn't you tell me where you were going? Why did you go over there at night? Susie, I cannot believe you would do something like this. I hope you have learned a lesson. Get your cell phone cancelled." On, and on he went.

Ms. Cox's daughter came home about an hour later. I am so thankful that we are all okay, and she had my phone. I can only imagine what my children will say about this. Casey said she did not leave with us because she knew what Mark might do to us. I couldn't understand why she would go in the first place, since she is afraid of Mark, but she went with other people, and he happened to be there.

I hadn't spoken to my girlfriend Doris in a while, so I called her.

"Hey, girlfriend, haven't heard from you in a while. Is it true? I heard that you and John are back together."

"Yes, it's true. I'm thanking God. Sorry, Doris, I haven't touched base with you. Girl, so much has been going on that I've hardly had time to breathe."

"You will never guess what happened to Ms. Cox and me.

"She said Susie, are you crazy? What a dumb thing to do."

"I know, but I had the Lord on my side."

"Alright, Ms. "Lord on your side". You need to be careful, girl. Something bad could have happened to you."

"Yes, I know, Doris. I am not taking this lightly. You are right. From now on, I will think before I act. You know how I am when someone is in trouble."

"Ms. Cox needs to put her foot on that girl's neck, Susie."

"Doris is a single mom, like I was, and it is hard raising young children these days. I thank God every day that my children are the wonderful young people they are. And I am going to have a one-on-one with her. I just finished giving her a gold star for the excellent job she has been doing; now this. I hate to have to kick her out of the group; she needs help. And I am trying to give that to her."

***"But the fruit of the spirit is love, joy, peace, gentleness, patience, goodness, faithfulness."* Galatians 5:22**

John and my children told us that we are out of our minds and taking all this a bit too far, especially me. Let the police manage it, they said. The police cannot save these young people. Parents have thrown them out in the streets. My daughter Valerie was so afraid for our family, especially me, and the police agreed, but we continued to teach them along with our Pastors. That is about all we could do for our young people: teach them the word of God and hope that they were listening. As soon as our grandchildren can read, we will start them reading the children's bible and telling them about our Lord and Savior. They are growing up so fast. We must keep them focused on the word of God. Most of the young people in our group have gone off to college or gotten married. All we can hope for is that they remember what we have tried to teach them.

***"With my whole heart have I sought the: Oh, let me not wander from thy commandments."* Psalm 119:10**

John and I are still doing God's work. We have a considerable number of new children in our group to replace those who have left. Our churches are growing rapidly. God still blesses us. My son Thomas finally married his fiancée, Barbara. The wedding was precious. The bride's family came, and we finally got to meet her mom and dad, and her sister, who was the Matron of Honor. My son was so happy, and his wife was glowing. They went to Mexico on their honeymoon. They decided to stay in New York and bought a house close to where my daughter lives. They also have jobs set up here. Thomas has a job as a bank administrator with Chase Bank, and Barbara's a nurse at the Mt. Sinai Hospital in East Harlem, New York. I am so happy that they are staying in town.

My husband and I have been so busy that we skipped our second anniversary. We did manage to have a little celebration at home, but this time we went to California to visit my sister Leslie, Bradley, and their little daughter. As you can imagine, family is a big part of John and my life; they mean the world to us. We cannot stop thanking God for our families.

CHAPTER 20
Another Addition To Our Family

We learned to take the good and the bad because after we returned home, we received some sad news. My cousin called to tell us that my uncle Fred had passed away. He was my favorite uncle; he was the one who called me Susie Q. So, we had to make a trip back to Kansas for the funeral. Uncle Fred lived a good life; he was a sweet man who loved the Lord. His wife, Aunt Doreen, is moving in with their daughter, Gracie, which is a good thing; she will not be alone at her age.

> **"For thou hast delivered my soul from death, mine eyes from tears, and my feet from falling." Psalm 116:8**

My goodness, Beth and Donald blessed our family with a new baby boy. Everyone is so happy for them. If you remember early on, she and Donald lost their only son in a pool accident, which almost destroyed our whole family. Can you see how good God is? Then, not long after, he blessed them with two more children.

My husband was feeling blessed. Their little son looks just like Raymond, and they named him Ryan, which means "little king." He is so precious.

We're still teaching our young people from church while trying to keep the gangs from taking over, and drugs out of our schools. We need to keep them close and surround them with prayer. All these drug dealers need is a curious young person to entrap.

My friends and I are so busy with work and our grandchildren that we hardly ever see each other, and we only call occasionally. My next-door neighbor, Ms. Grant, is still teaching me to crochet. I am about to finish my first wrap and am doing an exceptional job, so says Ms. Grant. I am ready for my next project, but my husband wants more time with our older grandchildren. They are growing up so fast and will soon prefer time with friends rather than us.

I just found out from the doctor that I am diabetic. My husband wants me to stop working so that I can take better care of myself and eat healthily. As we get older, we need to take better care of ourselves. We still do our regular walks as much as possible.

> **"My help comes from the Lord, the Maker of heaven and earth. He will not let your foot slip he who watches over you will not slumber;"** ***Psalm 121:2-3***

> **"All scripture is given by inspiration of God, and is profitable for doctrine, for reproof, for correction, for instruction in righteousness: That the man of God may be perfect, thoroughly furnished unto all good works."** ***2 Timothy 3:16-17***

This scripture teaches us the value of guiding others, children and adults alike, toward godly behavior, correcting wrongdoing, and helping one another return to our true, righteous selves.

CHAPTER 21
Remembering The Past

My cousin Gracie called to say Aunt Doreen wasn't doing well after Uncle Fred passed. I felt emotional, thinking about them and especially my parents, who struggled to give Herbert and me a good life. They rarely spoke about their parents, only saying they grew up very poor and wanted us to look forward, not back. I'll never forget that perspective.

That's why my parents moved us to Kansas so Herbert and I could have a fresh start. I love them for that. Pacing the floor, I shivered, missing Mom, Dad, and Herbert. Suddenly, a knock interrupted my thoughts: a local insurance salesperson. I told him I already had a policy and didn't want to discuss it today.

"Hmm, Susie, snap out of it," I told myself, then called my friend Doris. We hadn't spoken in a while.

"Hey friend, how are you?" She laughed.

"Not a darn thing, what about you?"

I admitted, "Just thinking about Mom and Dad."

"Don't let that get you down. Want me to come over?"

"No, my husband will be home soon. I need to pull myself together. Love you."

"Love you too, Susie. Say hi to John."

"Will do."

I just needed to tell someone how I felt, but I was alright. I cooked dinner for us. John arrived at five-thirty.

"Thanks, baby, for this wonderful dinner."

"Anything for my man." We laughed. I remembered falling for Josh, which was different. Loving John felt real and intimate, even without acting on it. Josh was all talk, dishonest and manipulative.

As I think about it, I didn't like the way my mother waited on my father, whom I love dearly, and my mom. But now with John, I find myself doing just that, waiting on him hand and foot. I realized that it is all about love. Mama loved Daddy, and she did not mind doing it for him out of love, especially if you are a stay-at-home spouse who does not work outside of the home, like most women do today. After work, a woman feels it is her spouse's responsibility to share in household chores. Now, like my daughter, she does not work outside the home, so she serves her husband's needs, but he helps her with the kids' care when she is busy. My friends and I expect our spouses to help us with household chores because we all work. They do not get to sit around watching football all day while we are cleaning, but we do get to have dinner out. I don't cook much unless I'm off work.

I just found out that some of our young people will be going off to college when school is out, and I'm so happy for their fresh starts. We always lose some each year. For example, Casey is heading to Mississippi State University, supported by family, and gaining independence from Mark. I hope she chooses to keep her new path private.

CHAPTER 22
Birthday Celebration

My husband's birthday is coming up, and I would like to do something special for him. I have never given him a surprise birthday party. He is going to be surprised; it must be elegant. I will encourage my children and John's children to help me pull this off. They are exceptionally good at doing things like this. But one thing I am worried about is that if our grands get a hold of it, it will be all over because they will surely tell grandpa. I am going to group text them all so they can come up with some great ideas for when we meet. I am getting excited already about this.

I will invite his brothers, my sister, and her husband, our friends, and people from his job; it is going to be big. Oh my, John will think I am taking him out to dinner as always. It is not far off, so we have to get on it. We need to get invitations printed, starting with the Venue, the Elegance Event Space, or Brooklyn Kouture House in Brooklyn, New York. My baby deserves the best. He is such a wonder man that he does not like being in the spotlight.

Ring, Ring, "Hello, hi Doris, what's going on over your way?"

"Oh, not much, I called to see what you were doing."

"I am over here reminiscing about John's birthday coming up very soon and what I would like to do."

"So, what did you come up with if I'm not being nosy?"

«I was thinking of a surprise party for him, but you know that is just the way he is; he does not want a lot of attention. But I am going to do it anyway. His birthday is in three weeks, so I have to work fast. What are you doing tomorrow after church?"

"You know the game will be on, and I can sneak away and meet with my kids, and you can come with me."

"Nothing that I know of, yes, I would love to, what time?"

"I'll have to let you know after I contact my kids to see if they can get away, someone has to keep the grandkids, because mum the word they will tell for sure." Doris laughed,

"Girl, I do know what you mean, they don't seem to keep anything from their papa."

"I was thinking about Kouture, or the Event Space."

"Yeah, I like them both, but the Kouture is a great place."

"Yes, that's what I was thinking too, I'll have to see what the kids think."

«And how do you anticipate getting John to go?» «I am taking him to dinner, and I wanted it to be a special place. He will not want to go there, but I will sweet-talk him into it. I will text you later tonight to let you know the time we need to work quickly, because time is essential.

"Okay, I'll bc waiting."

"Hello, Valerie. Did you get my text? Is it possible for us to meet at your house tomorrow after church during the game? Doris is coming to help me also, if you don't mind."

"Yes, Mama, that will be fine. Do the rest of them know?"

"No, I wanted to check with you first. Do you think Michael will be able to take the kids somewhere, because you know they will tell?"

"I'll ask him, maybe to the game room or a movie, but not too late, because they have school."

"Okay, honey, thanks. I have some plans I'll need y'all's opinion."

"Hello, son, what's going on over your way?"

"Nothing, Mom, just watching the games, what's up?"

"Oh, I wanted to know if you could meet at Valarie's tomorrow during the game after church. I know you want to see the game, but we can still have it on while discussing John's party?"

"Okay Mom, that will work. Tell Marcie, and you know the Kids can't be there, maybe Michael can take them with him and his kids. I also need to call Beth and Donald so they can figure out what to do with their kids. We probably need to get this finished because folks will start to get suspicious."

"Yes, Mama, you are right. See you tomorrow."

"Thanks, honey." "Hi Beth, what are you all doing over there?"

"Nothing, Mom, what's up with you?"

"Well, honey, I wanted to know if you or Donald could meet up with us tomorrow after church to plan a birthday party for your dad? I know the guys all want to see that game, and the kids can't come because they'll tell everything. So, whatever you can work out, hopefully this will be the only meeting we'll need, and I can handle the rest myself. So, if you can, I would appreciate it, you know your father's not going to like this, but I will sweet-talk him into it."

"Alright, Mom, one of us will be there."

"Thanks, my love."

Once I finish dinner, I will call John's brother, and he can contact the other. Then I will call my sister. After we got together on Sunday afternoon, our kids, Doris, and I accomplished a lot; we agreed on the place, the time, and the menu. So, all I had to do was call and set everything in motion. It was not going to be formal, just church attire. No gifts, it is going to be beautiful. After work on Tuesday, Doris and I went to the printer to order the invitations. John's birthday is quickly approaching on January 31, so we decided to have it on Saturday, February 1, at 4:00 pm. I have a friend who works with John, so I will have her take care of all his friends there. We will need a headcount and RSVPs very soon.

The celebration turned out great. I told John that I was taking him out to dinner for his birthday, and he wouldn't mind because that is what we always do.

I told him, "Honey, I am taking you to this wonderful place for a special dinner. I heard that it is a wonderful place just the two of us, no kids."

"Okay, honey, sounds wonderful."

I thought to myself, I hope he does not recognize anyone's car when we arrive. I was trying to distract him so he would not have time to look around. John was so surprised, he looked at me and said,

"Baby, no, you did not." He said,

"I noticed that you have been busy here lately."

I said, "Happy birthday, sweetheart. I love you."

He said, "I love you, too."

The celebration turned out beautifully, and everyone we invited was there. We had so much fun that our grandchildren were as excited as their grandpa.

We played music, danced, ate, and drank until the early hours of the morning. We had a special room for the children. They had all fallen asleep. We both thanked everyone for coming. John said, "I first want to thank my beautiful wife and my family for this wonderful surprise, because I was really surprised, and thank all of you." Then he started calling the names of people he worked with: Tony, Dale, Joyce, and, oh, my brothers Ben and Charles, my sisters in love, Joyce and Mary. Thank you all for coming. I love you.

Please eat and drink all this food. Take food home with you. A special thanks to my good friend and neighbor for her help. And my wonderful children. We had a glorious time, and everyone left happy. John was obviously pleased; he could not stop thanking me and telling me how much he loved me.

We did not make it to church on Sunday morning, but we had already invited our pastors, and they both declined. They had called to wish John a happy birthday early on. We were so tired that we did not even go to work on Monday. We took a vacation day off. You know, we are not as young as we used to be, plus we had company to entertain.

John was so happy that his brothers came that he could not believe it. He told me that at work on Tuesday, everyone was talking about the surprise party you gave me and how nice it was.

"It was good to hear that they enjoyed it and how wonderful you made it."

"Thank you again, baby."

"You're welcome, honey, nothing too good for my baby." We laughed.

Our young people's group got wind of the party and was telling me that they heard how great it was, everyone is talking about how you surprised Bro. Barter. Okay, girls, let us get back to our studies, and thanks for the updates. I have a loving bunch of young ladies. I enjoy studying with them because I learn right along with them.

Such joy. Now I understand what my husband meant when he talked about being a good example for them and how much he loved these young men, because I feel the same kind of love for the young ladies.

CHAPTER 23
John's Illness

I am so happy, God is blessing our family every day, and I thank Him. I am so busy doing all kinds of things. For example, tonight my husband is working late, and he stays busy as well. So, my girls and I decided to have a girls' night out for dinner. We had so much fun. Tomorrow, my young ladies' group will be going to our favorite senior living home to read scriptures, pray, and sing with them. We even play games with them. We do this monthly.

Although we are busy doing other things, we set aside time just for ourselves. We are both getting older and cannot do the things that we have enjoyed over the years. I have also noticed that my sweet, sweet husband has not been as active as usual; he has been so tired lately. I have tried to get him to see the doctor. We made an appointment. I couldn't predict what the doctor might tell him, since he is never ill. I was so worried, all I could do was pray and hope for the best. The doctor ran so many tests, and we had to wait for the results, which was hard.

We made an appointment for next week, which was the longest week of our lives. I could see that my husband was worried about what the doctor would tell him. His energy and his appetite were not what they used to be. He had talked about my retiring and taking care of myself, but now he is talking about both of us retiring and spending more time with the family. That really took me by surprise.

The day finally came for us to get the results of the tests. When the doctor came in, he said to John that it was bad news, but it could be treated. My heart fell to the floor. He told us that John has a bad kidney disease. My friend, you need a Kidney transplant. In the meantime, I am putting you on the transplant list, but we can check people that you know, family, friends, etc., to see if we can find a donor that is willing to help you.

John said, "Oh no, how long do I have if I cannot find a donor?"

The doctor told John, "We are not going to worry about that right now. Just eat healthily, exercise, and I have medication for you to take. Also, I will be putting you on dialysis, which will be twice a week starting tomorrow morning."

We drove home very quietly. We called the children over and explained what was going on with their father. They all agreed to get an evaluation right away, as I knew they would. Lord, please let someone be a match for my baby. I cannot lose him now. We still have so much to live for: grandchildren to see grow up and become parents. We called our Pastor and went to his office to talk to him. Of course, he prayed for us. He said, "Stay in prayer. You know that God can do all things. Trust Him the way you have been doing."

After the first dialysis treatment, John was ill, but as time passed, he felt better. The doctor mentioned that people experience post-treatment illness. I asked John if it was time for him to retire so he could heal, and I would continue to work to keep things going. Then, when he was well enough, I would retire, and we could travel.

Of course not, he said, "No way am I going to just give up my life until his Heavenly Father calls me home. We're going to be alright, honey. I do not want you to worry about me. We're going to continue our lives as usual with just a few setbacks."

So that is just what we did. We prayed a lot, I cried, I couldn't help it - I just didn't let him see me. We both continued to work, but I could tell that his energy was getting less. When he got home each day, he would be so tired that he sometimes fell asleep on the sofa before dinner.

> ***"But thou, O Lord, art a God full of compassion, and gracious, long suffering, and plenteous in mercy and truth. O turn unto me and have mercy upon me; give thy strength unto thy servant, and save the son of thine handmaid."*** **Psalm 86:15-16**

The children are all worried that none of them are donors, and no one from the list has come forward. My neighbors have all been evaluated. Please, Lord, there must be someone out there who's a match. Yet, John goes on with life day after day, and he tries to be upbeat. He goes to work every day and sometimes he seems so tired. However, thankfully, he's still able to go for our evening walks that we've been doing for years. God keeps giving him the strength to keep on going, and I'm thankful because that keeps me from hovering over him with pity, which I'm trying so hard not to do if he can deal with all he's going through, so can I. I have too.

CHAPTER 24

John's Treatment Continues

We went to church on Sunday. At first, John didn't want to go, and I didn't want to go without him. Because of that, he decided to come. Once we arrived, everyone was excited to see him, and we both felt blessed. This happiness gave us the strength for our meeting with the young people, who were thrilled that we had come. John said being surrounded by their hugs lifted his spirits from his earlier reluctance. My young woman made me feel loved, and the good meeting ended with their mother's small celebration to welcome me back.

It does not seem like John is getting any better. He has lost so much weight, but his appetite is still excellent; I am happy about that. I considered consulting another specialist, but I know he will not go because he trusts Doctor Burns. And still, there have not been any matches. The list is so long that I worry my baby's running out of time. I am afraid, but I cannot let John know how I feel. I do not need him worrying about me, too. He is still working, and I can see that it is taking its toll on him. I wish I could get him to retire, but he says it does not matter where I am when God gets ready for me. And I said, "Please, honey, do not talk like that." I am so glad that I had that birthday celebration for him and did not wait. I feel like my husband's not going to be with me much longer, and when I think about it, I can't breathe.

I want him to stop working, but he says he isn't ready, as he wants to prove he can still do these things. I thank God for his courage; John is ***very*** proud. Sometimes his daughter Beth can persuade him. I'll see if she can convince him to retire or work part-time. His desk job isn't hard physically, but it's mentally draining.

"Lord, I pray that you will keep your loving arms around my husband all the days of his life. Lord Jesus, you know that John is a loving, affectionate, and God-fearing man; he loves you, Lord. He's worried about those young men that he ministers to each week. He doesn't want to leave them unattended. Oh Lord, keep him lifted up. Oh Heavenly Father, I can't depend on anyone but you, Lord, that's why I'm coming to you in the most humble way I know how. Father, You said to call on You, and You will hear and answer prayer. I know you will, because you've done it before, and you can do it again. We know of Your loving kindness, and we trust You in all things. I know that we can't do anything without Your will. Thank You, Lord Jesus, for what You have done for this family and what You're going to do. You've been with me and seen me through so many things. I don't know where I would be today if it weren't for Your grace and mercy. I love you, Lord. I pray that you keep your arms around my husband all the days of his life. Watch over John and his children, grandchildren, and great-grandchildren. And Lord, please have mercy on me, his wife, and we'll be careful to give you all the praise and glory, for it is in Your darling Son Jesus' Name that I pray this prayer." Amen.

CHAPTER 25

John Goes To The Hospital

It worries me that John has the same disease my father died from. I haven't told the children, not wanting to burden them. Lately, John seems more tired and urinates more, but I thought it was just from working too much. I try not to press him to do the things we used to do daily, like staying home or going to the lake. Today, he saw the babies at his daughter's house, and the children come by daily to help. I'm grateful for our children.

Earlier today, John's job called to tell me he had passed out at work and was being taken to the hospital. In that moment, I almost lost my mind. When I arrived, they were running lots of tests on him, and I could not see him for a long time; I was frantic. I called the children, and they all showed up. Their presence was such a relief to me. The grandchildren kept checking in to ask if grandpa was all right. Later, when his co-workers got off work, they stopped by the hospital. Friends, neighbors, and our Pastor and his wife, who are so fond of John, also came.

Finally, after what felt like hours, they let me in to see him, along with our Pastor, and that was that no one else. He was so glad to see us. I could see the fear in my baby's eyes. He settled down when Pastor Berry began to pray for him. I was trying to contain myself so that John would not know just how upset I was. After the Pastor prayed, he went out to talk to everyone, but I stayed with John. Later that evening, the staff told me to go home and get some rest, because John needed it too. Of course, I told them that I am not leaving him here alone. They said, "We're sorry, Mrs. Barter, but you will have to." "We'll keep you informed on his progress," they assured me. That's when John said, "Baby, please go home. I'll be alright. Get some rest. I'll try to call you later tonight before you go to sleep."

After leaving the hospital with my family, I stayed at my daughter's house, but I could not sleep. I tossed and turned, cried, and prayed all night long. As soon as morning came, I went to the hospital to check on John. They told me that he had a restless night, but he was finally asleep, and I could sit with him quietly.

My baby looked so tired and pale; it just broke my heart to see him like that. He slept for a long time. When he woke up, he saw me and smiled.

He said, "Hi, baby."

"Hi, yourself. How are you feeling?"

"I'm okay. Don't you worry about me, I'll be fine. You don't look like you got any sleep, am I right?" he asked me.

"I'm alright, honey, I am just worried about you." Doctor Burns came in.

"Hello John, how are you doing this morning?"

"Oh, doc, I should be asking you that—how am I doing?"

"John, I want to get some more tests done as soon as you finish eating breakfast."

"Doc, just do the tests. I am not hungry."

"You need something in your stomach. You haven't eaten anything since you've been here. The tests can wait, and I'll be back after I get the result, alright?"

"Yes, alright, doc."

After breakfast, John fell asleep again. Later that morning, we woke him for the test. While he was away, our daughters arrived at the hospital. I told them I was worried about the results, especially since Dr. Burns ordered more tests because John was still not okay.

"Momma, are you okay? You look tired, and I know you didn't sleep last night. I heard you moving around."

"Yes, baby, I am a little tired. Did anyone call his brothers? I have not had a chance." "Don't worry, Greg called them. He'll keep them updated and mentioned he'll see John when he gets off work."

"How are my grandchildren?"

"They're good. They ask how grandpa is and whether he'll be alright. We say yes and pray for him."

"I haven't ceased from praying since this happened."

"Mom, have you eaten? Valerie asked. Beth and I can get ourselves lunch while John's gone."

"I probably could eat, maybe a salad and iced tea."

When John finally got back from his tests, he looked more stressed than when he left. "How are you feeling, baby?" I asked.

"Not particularly good. I need to take a nap."

"Go ahead and sleep, baby. Valerie and Beth came up to see you. They went to get us some lunch. They'll be right back, but you go on and sleep. I love you."

"I love you too."

John didn't wake up until late evening. After the boys visited, the girls went home and tried to convince me to leave, but I couldn't. I might try staying the night, though John will probably want me to go home. Still, I can't rest away from him. He ate a little dinner without much appetite, but he was happy to see the kids. We have wonderful children.

That night, John was restless again and did not sleep well at all; of course, neither did I. We talked for a while before he fell asleep. He told me how much he loved me, our family, and our life together. He kept repeating, "I enjoyed every moment of it."

"You know I love you too, and I feel the same way, baby, but try and get a little rest. We can talk later." I was so grateful they allowed me to stay the night. In the middle of the night, he suddenly jumped up:

"Tell my brothers that I love them."

"Baby, I will tell them," I assured him. It scared me so badly that I had to go outside the room. I knew he was leaving; I could feel him slipping away. Oh God, please do not take him away. Everything was shutting down, Doctor Burns explained. My boys did not go home. They stopped as they ran over to me:

"Mom, Mom, what is the matter?" I was so hysterical that I could not speak.

"It's your dad, he's saying goodbye. I know he is." My son Greg went in to see him, but he was asleep.

CHAPTER 26

Last Night Was John's Final Night

Before daylight, my husband passed away in his sleep. My heart ached. Losing John was the hardest thing I've faced. What will I do now?

The boys got things straightened out at the hospital, called the girls to tell them about their dad, and let them know they were bringing me home. I did not want to go over to Valerie's house—I just wanted to go home and be with John. But they didn't want me to be alone, so they took me home and stayed until the girls arrived. When the house filled up with all the children, grandchildren, Pastor Falconer, Pastor Berry, and their wives, the atmosphere shifted: everyone prayed for us, and soon we were all crying together. It was overwhelming; no one could comfort themselves or each other.

The next few days were just as hard. We had to plan John's funeral and inform everyone. I was grateful to God for our children—they worked miracles and got things done. Our young people came to help, brought food, made sure I ate, sat with me, and prayed. They were wonderful. Our grandchildren, grown up now, helped and cared for me.

John's brothers arrived with their wives and children. I was glad to see them.

The house was full of people until I went to my bedroom to be alone. John's brother Benjamin came up to comfort me. We both cried together. Later, his wife Joyce came up, and they locked the door so we could be alone. They are such good people, like their brother John.

My sister Leslie and her husband Bradley arrived a few days later, and I noticed their children had grown so much. In addition, even my cousins from Kansas came to the funeral, which made me happy.

Today was such a long, exhausting day. I did not think I would be able to get through it, but with the help of the All-Mighty God and His grace and mercy, I did. Our children had planned a wonderful celebration of life for John, befitting the life he lived. Everything was perfect. Reverend Falconer spoke a wonderful word for him. He loved John very much; he could hardly do the Eulogy but thank God he did. My baby looked so peaceful, as if he were asleep. I appreciate my neighbors, friends, and colleagues. They prepared the repast. Thank God for them! Everything was beautiful.

When it was over, I was so alone. The only thing that kept me upright was my children, grandchildren, neighbors, and friends, who made sure that I was not left on my own. Although I miss John deeply and always will, I also feel grateful for the support that surrounds me. To get through this, I pray and ask God for strength.

I have been blessed to find true love. My second husband was truly the love of my life. Though we had no children together, we both had children from previous marriages and loved them all. We became a big, happy blended family.

CHAPTER 27

John's Home Going Celebration

We cherished our grandchildren with all our hearts, but we lost our oldest grandchild in an accident. The accident almost destroyed our family, but by the grace of God, we made it through.

Now we're dealing with the loss of my sweet partner and friend, whom I will love for the rest of my life. I have decided to continue working with the young people at our church because that is what John would want me to do. He would love for his work with the young men to continue. I'm going to ask John's oldest son, Paul, to continue his father's work. I have also decided to continue working on my job for as long as I can. I want to stay close to both my children and John's children, grandchildren, and great-grandchildren, watching them grow into young men and women. Greg Jr. will be graduating from college soon, and he has been dating this young lady, and I expect them to get married. In the meantime, I plan to stay busy working for the Lord and being there for my family and friends. I plan to travel, which I love.

After everything had settled down, I had the task of going through some of John's things. He had a small safe that he kept locked. I didn't think much about it, because he had been married before. I thought maybe he still had some of his late wife's things that he was keeping for the children. So, I never asked him about it. But when I opened the box, I could not believe what I saw inside. My sweet, loving God-fearing husband had a secret that ripped my heart from my chest. I couldn't believe what I saw. He had a secret that no one would ever believe.

I screamed and cried all night long. The man I loved so much, after fifteen years of marriage, has kept a big secret from me. Oh God, what am I going to do about this? No one would ever believe it, because I don't believe it myself. O God, how could he? How could he do this to me, to our family? I know that John loved the Lord; how could he not? He had gotten trapped in a situation that he couldn't get away from. He was a good man. How could I love him if he weren't? How long will I be able to keep this to myself? But I have to for the sake of our children. Did he even tell his brothers about this? Lord Jesus, please help me to live with this. As I prayed, I remembered this song by DJ Roger's, "God Favors Me." Again, I'll rise because God favors me. Yes, I will rise again."

About the Author

My name is Pairlee (Pearlie) McGowan. I am an eighty-year-old mother of four, grandmother of eight, and great-grandmother of four, with another on the way.

My story blends fiction with truth, written from love of storytelling and a desire to share an important message. At its heart, this story is about how love, love of God, family, and friends, gives meaning to our lives and helps us endure.

This story follows a family that endured hardship by leaning on faith, a hardworking father, and a caring mother. Despite poverty, we always had shelter, food, and a church, shaping our character. Even when I disagreed as a child, I respected the guidance and upbringing I received.

As an adult, I've tried to pass these lessons to my children and grandchildren. Sadly, much family history is now harder to find, and I know some of you may relate.

I am blessed with children, grandchildren, and great-grandchildren, whom I love deeply. We suffered a terrible loss when one of our grandchildren and his son died in an accident. He was our oldest grandchild; his son was one of my great-grandsons. That loss nearly destroyed us, but by God's grace, we endure. The pain lingers, but we rely on God as we learn to live with it.

Thank God. May He bless you. Always remember to pray and keep Him first in your life.

www.ingramcontent.com/pod-product-compliance
Ingram Content Group UK Ltd.
Pitfield, Milton Keynes, MK11 3LW, UK
UKHW022019190726
13853UKWH00005B/2002